In the Blink of an Eye
The Reincarnations of Michael Kenney

In the Blink of an Eye

The Reincarnations of Michael Kenney

Kenneth M. Krakaur

Bujew
Press

In the Blink of an Eye
The Reincarnations of Michael Kenney

For further information, please contact:
Kenneth M. Krakaur at bujewpress@gmail.com.

Cover and book design by Tom Crockett
tomcrockett@mac.com

Printed in the United States of America

In the Blink of an Eye
The Reincarnations of Michael Kenney
Kenneth M. Krakaur

1. Title 2. Author 3. Fiction

ISBN: 978-0-9801860-1-7

Dedication

To my wife, Priscilla, who puts up with my sailing and writing obsession.

To my children, Rachel and Allison, who have shared many days sailing on *Last Call* and *Instant Karma*.

To my grandson Andrew, who always brings a smile to my face.

To the Peters family, Scarborough, South Africa, who helped me along the way, and

To those who have wondered about their lives—past, present and future.

Special Thanks

To Denise Peters, Scarborough, South Africa, contributing poet (Audrey's poem) and technical advisor.

Part One
The Past

*"Of all the elements of time,
it is the past that is the most tangible."*

Chapter 1

Flash

Blink, blink. Flash. Blink, flash. Blink, flash. Blink, flash. Thousands of times a day we blink and with each blink there is a sliver of darkness that is created as the eyelid passes over the pupil. Most people don't see the sliver or choose to ignore it. Some people have a nervous habit which makes their eyelids stay down longer. Their darkness is more than a sliver. Yet they don't see the darkness as they are too self-conscious about how long their blink is taking.

I saw my first flash when I was 8 years old. As I look back into my childhood, I remember that day as one of the most important days in my life.

In the Blink of an Eye

I was riding on a yellow school bus. The air was full of noise created by childish chatter. I stared out the window as we passed a line of pine trees. The speed of the bus against the tree trunks created a brown blur. Then I blinked and saw a flash, an image flash. The image was a face of a middle-aged man. He had blond hair, blue eyes, with a scar that crossed his cheek. He looked Scandinavian. I named him Sven, a name borrowed from my father's Swedish auto mechanic that tended to his 1960 Saab model 92, a car that needed constant attention. Several years later I determined that the man seen in the image flash was a Swedish man named Erick Alexson. He was a tall man. During the image flashes I found myself looking up at him as seen only through the eyes of a small child staring up at an adult. In some of the flashes I could see a woman standing next to him. And sometimes there was a girl. The girl must have been the daughter of these two people. So often in my image flashes I would see her staring at me, her eyes glued to my eyes. She had a shy smile, which I found comfortable and appealing. And then there was the word "Jost." Sometimes the word was spoken softly and sometimes it was said as if someone was ordering another person to do something.

Over the years I learned to regulate the flashes. When I was tired the flashes increased in frequency. When it was dark they also appeared more often.

Flash

And when it was light or bright they rarely occurred. I remember during my days playing Little League, I worried about getting a flash at the moment the pitcher released the ball. As the catcher, I could not miss catching a single pitch. At the start of each game I would eat several candy bars hoping that the sugar rush would keep me alert. In all the years of catching I only had one flash. And at that moment the ball hit me in the face mask right in front of my chin. The coach yelled out to me.

"Open your eyes, Michael." If he only knew.

When I was 10 years old I made another discovery. This is when I came to realize that people see images when they dream. I do not. Instead, I hear sounds and words. Sometimes the words are not in English, yet I know exactly what is being said. The first words I heard were eerie and terrifying. It was the voice of a young girl. I could hear her so clearly. "No, Papa. No, Papa. Please, Papa. Nooooo…" The next sound was a deafening blast, like that coming from a large rifle. Then there was another blast. It sounded like an echo from the first. Each time I had the dream I would force myself to wake up. Then I would notice a small wet spot on my shoulder. I would rub my fingers through it and taste it. I knew the taste. It was the taste of tears; children's tears. And as the thousands of flashes occurred over my life, I was able to connect them to my dream sounds until detailed stories emerged.

By the time I was 20 years old I had assembled incredible detail about two past events. These events which varied in length from days to years all had one common element. There was always one person in the story who had a very distinctive characteristic, whether the person was a man, a boy or a girl. We shared this defining characteristic, and it was that and only that which made me realize that we were undeniably linked.

Chapter 2

Birth after Death

Mankeeper and Ladykeeper were the secret names I had for the people who raised me. They adopted me shortly after the death of my real parents which preceded my birth by one month.

Stephen Kenney and Anne Barron grew up in Elizabeth City County, Virginia, in the 1940s. It was a time in Virginia's history that favored racial segregation. Stephen and Anne came from affluent families, who lived in large stately homes that had Sunset Creek as their backyard. The Kenneys' family wealth came from real estate. The Barron family made their money from banking and retail.

In the Blink of an Eye

While both families lost much of their wealth during the Depression, they retained their social status and their waterfront homes. By the time Stephen and Anne were married, all their parents had died. Early deaths seem to plague the Kenney and Barron families. Stephen and Anne were college graduates. My father was an engineer who also had a master's degree in business. My mother was a nurse who worked at a local hospital in the city of Hampton. There were a lot of dollars spent educating two people who died so young.

Stephen and Anne were childhood sweethearts whose families were close friends. They were sailing families who spent much of the summer months sailing and cruising on the Chesapeake Bay. Stephen was also an avid racer and an active member of the Hampton Yacht Club. He raced both small and large boats. Over the years he had accumulated extensive racing victories. He was well known up and down the Chesapeake Bay as the racer to beat. And while his love and passion for sailing were documented in numerous newspaper articles, he failed to pass on to me the skill and knowledge that would have made me a better racer.

On November 10, 1962, Stephen and Anne were out on the bay sailing their 27-foot wooden sloop. The day was one of those frequent days on the Chesapeake Bay that was so perfect that you could not distinguish the season. My mother was

Birth after Death

eight months pregnant. Near the end of the day as my father was preparing the boat for return to the marina, a speeding powerboat struck their sailboat, broadside. The ignited fuel from the powerboat generated a huge explosion that killed my father instantly. My mother was thrown from the boat and in the process her head smashed against the mast, snapping her neck.

Another boat raced to the scene and rescued my near-dead mother. She was transported to a trauma center in Norfolk, Virginia, where she was placed on life support awaiting my birth. On December 10, 1962, I was surgically and mechanically extracted from Anne. I remember seeing the light and feeling the chill of the air as my mother's belly was opened. I could feel the odd texture of the rubber surgical gloves. I could feel the pinch as they cut my cord. And as I took my first breath of hospital air, the ventilator was unplugged and Anne took her last breath. This was how I was brought into the world.

Sometimes when I dream I can hear the sound of the racing speedboat. I can hear my father yell out to Anne. I hear the explosion and later the sound of the monitors in the ICU beeping and beeping. And in the flashes I see the speedboat and the fireball and the destruction that happened on that beautiful day in November.

Not a day has gone by where I have not longed

In the Blink of an Eye

for my parents. Children should never have to lose their mother and father the way I lost Anne and Stephen. From what Mankeeper and Ladykeeper have told me, my parents were wonderful people. They were special people. And while I have asked the Keepers so many times about what made them so special, I have never gotten a straight answer. For that reason alone, I've always wondered if my parents saw flashes or had visionless dreams. I guess I'll never know.

Chapter 3

The Bujew

As I moved through adolescence, I started to keep records of my past lives. This is when I learned how to invoke flashes. I found two methods that yielded the best results. The first method involved watching snow; not the white stuff that falls from the sky but rather the white and black speckles you see on a TV when there is no broadcast on a given station. I would stare just for a few seconds and then begin blinking. The blinking needed to be rhythmic and regular. And as long as I kept up the rhythm the flashes would occur.

The other method was to lie on my bed and stare at the ceiling light as the ceiling fan turned

In the Blink of an Eye

slowly. I would dim the light and start blinking until the flashes became regular. Each session lasted five minutes and in that time I saw amazing images. Despite the almost addictive process I would force myself to stop. Then I would pick up my notebooks and record my images. Sometime my notes were very general, other times very detailed. By the time I entered college I had completed 30 composition notebooks, all written in small cursive lettering utilizing both sides of the page. All throughout the years I never shared my discoveries with anyone, until now.

Within the pages of my notebooks I also discussed the unique aspects of my upbringing. My keepers Su and Allen Stern were close friends of my parents. I don't know if I was adopted through a normal legal process or how I got from womb to room. But in the 1960s adoption guidelines in the South were very loose. Strangely enough, I was never given the name of my adoption parents; rather, they gave me the name of my real parents who died on the sailboat prior to my birth.

Su and Allen came together during the end of the Korean War. Su, an American war bride, was of medium height, fit, a beautiful Korean woman whose command of the English language came quickly. It was easy to understand how Allen fell in love with her. Her voice was so tender and she moved as gracefully as wheat blowing on an Eng-

The Bujew

lish hillside. She treated me like a son she naturally bore. And while I knew she wasn't my real mother, I loved her the way that most children love their mothers. Allen was also a terrific parent. We did all the typical father-son activities. We played baseball and basketball. We fished, we hunted and we sailed. Oh yes, we sailed. This is what fathers and sons did in Hampton Roads in the 1960s and '70s. This is also what Allen did as a personal commitment to Stephen and Anne.

Su and Allen were a Bujew couple and I was their Bujew son. Bujews are people who believe in the union of two bodies of teaching. The faith is anchored in Judaism and Buddhism, one religion and one non-religion. In Buddhism there is no God, only the belief in the teacher, the Buddha. Buddha was the first to admit that he was not a god and all the reincarnations of him have held to the same truth. It is said that Buddhism is the perfect religion for atheists.

Several times a year Su would take me to Washington, D.C., to visit the Buddhist temple. At the time, Washington was the closest place for Su and me to engage in our faith. During each trip we would spend hours learning the teachings of the Buddha and in some trips Su would also teach me about the art of meditation. Later on in life my meditation gave way to intentional image flashing.

During the Hebrew holy days we celebrated the

In the Blink of an Eye

traditional Hebrew rituals and while Allen did not normally attend weekly services at the synagogue, his faith and commitment to Judaism were strong. I remember feeling so lucky to have two faiths to follow, both anchored in the tradition of wisdom and compassion. So often Allen and Su would tell me that my life should be anchored by the 13 principles of their faiths. The 13 principles of the Bujew: The Ten Commandments, the Wisdom and the Compassion fundamentals of Buddhism, and the Golden Rule.

Chapter 4

The Shack

When I turned 16, Allen surprised me with my first car. It was a very used Saab two-seater. The car was yellow, had a fiberglass body, and a four-speed manual transmission. It was quirky and like my father's Saab, required the constant attention of Sven. I kept the car through college. At age 17, I graduated from high school and began my college career at the College of William and Mary. I decided to commute to school, a decision that proved to be very beneficial to the process of discovering my past. I also wanted to stay close to home and close to my boat, a 22-foot knockabout that was built by a small boatyard on Sunset Creek.

In the Blink of an Eye

College life at William and Mary was simple for commuter students. The war in Vietnam was over and college campuses were no longer a hotbed of student discontent and unrest. I took my learning responsibilities fairly seriously once I decided on my major. I started out in business and hated that. I tried math--that was not a good match--and finally settled into English and philosophy. (So Bujew.)

Dating also took up a lot of time. There were many dates; most were fun, and while I never let many get too close to me, one did sneak in. Her name was Audrey. She was a woman who I thought I could love forever. Audrey was very special. She had long streaked blonde hair that she wore straight, parted in the middle, hanging six inches below her shoulder. Her ears flared out just enough to part her hair on each side, a look I still like today. She was fit, pretty and smart. Everything about her was beautiful. But she was also way too perceptive and intuitive. This became a concern for me. She was able to see inside me in a way that made me feel very vulnerable.

Audrey was also a commuter student. She lived with her father in Charles City County on a farm the family had purchased in the pre-World War I era. The farm was named Houghton Plantation. It was originally named by a British farmer who settled the plantation in the early 1800s. His name

The Shack

was Robert Paulson. He had come to America from Houghton, West Sussex, England.

The first time I went to Houghton Plantation was with Audrey. It was November and the day was cold and gray. The long driveway to the house was lined with cypress trees. The air should have smelled like pine but instead smelled like old sweat, the type of smell that infiltrated the T-shirt of a tired, overworked laborer. Then I blinked and an image filled the sliver of darkness. A girl, a black girl, kneeled over another black person, possibly a boy. We continued to drive until we came to the house.

Audrey grabbed my hand. "Michael, are you okay?" Somehow she saw the terror in my eyes.

"Yeah, I'm okay."

"Come on, let me show you around." Her voice sounded distant. We parked the car and walked around the side yard through a small unkempt garden. The house had two stories, with white painted brick. The two chimneys were extra tall and looked out of place. The glass in the windows was old, discolored and distorted. Any attempt to see inside was blocked by the white sheer curtains that hung in the windows. The roof was made of red slate that was tinted green from the algae and moss that grew on it. The algae growth thrived because of large shadows that were cast upon the roof by the 100-foot hardwood trees that surrounded the

In the Blink of an Eye

house of Houghton Plantation.

The ground was covered with gold leaves and had a spongy feel underfoot. There were six small shacks that lined the edge of the backyard. "Audrey, what are those buildings about?"

"My father said they were slave shacks. That's where the slaves lived before the war." A lump grew in my throat.

"Michael, I have to use the bathroom. I'll be right back."

"Sure, no problem." Alone in the yard, I walked to the shack in front of me. The door was unlocked. I opened it slowly. It was empty. The smell of sweat and death came over me. My eyes started to blink and then images appeared. The little black girl I had seen during the drive down the driveway was crying. The boy she was tending to was facedown. There were cuts on his back. They were bleeding. I tried to stop blinking but the images seemed to be controlling me. Then the girl turned her head and looked directly at me. I forced my eyes open, not allowing myself to blink.

"Michael, Michael." I spun around to see Audrey standing behind me. "My God, are you okay? You looked possessed. What did you see?"

"Nothing, Audrey. Look, I have to go." And with that said, I walked to my car. As I got in, I could hear Audrey yelling, "Michael, what did you see?"

The Shack

That night I dreamed and the only sounds I could hear were screams punctuated by snapping sounds. The snapping sounds came from a whip.

After that day, Audrey became more and more fascinated with me until her fascination became overly uncomfortable. Over the next 18 months we were together, I never returned to Houghton Plantation. I didn't need to. I had seen all that I needed to see that single day. As spring approached, Audrey's sense of me had grown to the point that I actually feared her. She was on to me and my addiction. She knew I was seeing things and hearing things, and I knew if I didn't end the relationship, she would eventually confront me, and I didn't want to allow that to happen.

The last time I saw Audrey was two weeks before graduation. I remember the last time I kissed her, not because of the kiss but because of what she said to me after the kiss. "Don't let the demons get you, Angel." She never called me Angel. Later it was revealed to me in my dreams that the black girl in the shack was a slave named Angel Lehcar.

Audrey never showed up for graduation. Her name was called but there was no Audrey. A week later I drove by Houghton Plantation. The lawn hadn't been mowed for months and there was a "For Sale" sign hanging on a post. The sign gave no agent's name or phone number.

In the Blink of an Eye

Chapter 5

Lawyers, Locks
and Keys

Lawyers are like locks and keys. They exist only because some people in the world are dishonest. Remove the dishonest people and you can throw away the locks, the keys, and the lawyers. Every town has a lawyer or two, or a hundred. Big towns and cities have more lawyers than doctors. Lawyers occupy more space in the Yellow Pages than any other advertiser. In Hampton, Virginia, there were many lawyers, one who played a very important role in the life of Anne and Stephen. Edward Dermott was a well-educated, compassionate and wise man, who had befriended the Sterns. He went by the nickname Mickey Dermott. I shortened it to Mick

In the Blink of an Eye

Dermott. I always addressed him as Mick Dermott as if it was the last name McDermott. Mick Dermott specialized in real estate, regular estates and surreal estate. He was not only the lawyer for the Sterns but also for Sun Engineering where both Allen and Stephen worked.

Stephen was not a risk taker. He bought insurance for every possible risk. As an executive at Sun he had a fairly good benefit package. The package included life insurance calculated at four times salary. But with a baby on the way, four times salary was not enough. At the urging of my father, Mick Dermott had secured another policy, which paid double the face value in the event of an accidental death. The policy had a face value of $500,000. None of this was known to me until I graduated from college.

Mick Dermott had another job. He looked after the Sterns, who looked after me. All this was spelled out in the will. Each month Su and Allen got a visit from Mick Dermott. Most of the time they had dinner at our home. I sat at the table during dinner, but each time after dessert was served, I was asked to leave. This is when they discussed the cost of raising me and it was when money should have been exchanged. All of this was included in the will. And while Su and Allen were certainly entitled to fair compensation, they never accepted a dime.

Lawyers, Locks and Keys

After graduation and just before my 22nd birthday, I received a phone call from Mick Dermott. He suggested I come to his office for a visit to discuss issues concerning my parent's estate. It never occurred to me that my parents had an estate.

Mick Dermott's office was very basic; no frills for Mick Dermott. He was way too practical. He greeted me in the lobby, put his arm around my shoulder and escorted me into a conference room. "Michael, come and have a seat. This is my legal assistant, Judy Keyfa. She will be serving as a witness today."

"Why do we need a witness, Mick Dermott?"

"You'll understand in a few minutes." Then Mick Dermott opened a file and pulled out copies of all the news articles about the boating accident, the police investigation report, a copy of my parents' will and the insurance policies. There was also a letter from the Kenneys to their children. Over the next several hours I learned more about my parents than I had known in the last 22 years, and when all was said and done and all the papers were signed, I emerged from Mick Dermott's office a wealthy man. The only thing that was not discussed was the letter.

My father's Sun Engineering policy paid $300,000. The other policy paid $500,000 for death and $500,000 because his death was acci-

In the Blink of an Eye

dental. The $1.3 million had been invested, and more than doubled over the years. My net worth was slightly over $3 million, $2 million after the $1 million I would give to Su and Allen. At 22 years old with $2 million, one could follow two paths. One was the path to self-indulgence and the other was the path to wisdom and compassion. Because of my Bujew upbringing, I chose the latter. There was no need for a paying job but there was a need to make the world a better place.

The only feeling I had as I walked back to my car was numbness. My mind was spinning. I was on information overload. I sat in my car with my head leaned back, the letter lying on my lap, still unopened. The letter consisted of a single sheet of paper, folded in thirds, and sealed with a single staple in the middle of the page. I pried off the staple and opened the letter. I let it sit on my lap as I was afraid to read it. I stared at the blue sky through the windshield and started to blink and after a few seconds I saw my father writing the letter, the stapler next to his right hand. I watched him write it, fold it and staple it. Then the images stopped and I realized it was time to read the letter. The letter was titled "The Family Will and Tontine."

Dear Children,

If you are reading this tontine then it is a sad day for all of us. The tontine was to terminate

Lawyers, Locks and Keys

when the youngest child reached majority age. If this document is in your hand, then I'm so sorry we were unable to fulfill our parental commitments. Please forgive us. Depending upon the timing of our deaths this tontine may be worth a lot of money. Our wish is that you use it wisely. There are so many people in the world that can benefit from your generosity. Make it your life's work. Have a wonderful life. We will be joined together on the other side.

Love,
Dad and Mom

The letter was so brief. They never really thought it would be read. How wrong they were.

I continued to sit in my car and started to think about Audrey and wished for a moment that she was beside me in my yellow Saab sports car. I missed her voice, her smile and the smell of her hair. If she just had not tried so hard to get inside my head we could still be together. But my desire for Audrey was not to be fulfilled. Not now anyway.

The drive home should have taken minutes but instead took an hour. I drove to Grandview and sat in my car staring at the bay. I felt an odd presence about me, as if a version of me was sitting beside me. I closed my eyes and started to dream. "Jost, I'm afraid. Help me. I'm so cold."

In the Blink of an Eye

Then I forced my eyes open only to find the wet spot on my shoulder.

Chapter 6

Jost:
Coming to America

"No, Papa. No, Papa. Please, Papa. Nooooooo…"
And at that moment, the barrel of Papa's long rifle
was lowered and fired. The bullet accelerated from
the rifle's barrel at the speed of sound and flew 50
yards until it found a lung, a lung of a four-year-
old doe. Sonnet flew into my arms, "Why did he
have to do that?" She began sobbing, her tears
saturating my shirt.

Sonnet was too sensitive and too much a girl
to be able to watch my father kill another deer.
With each kill, there were Sonnet hysterics. Deer
meat was a staple for our family. It was plentiful
and we were poor. Sonnet's face stayed buried in

In the Blink of an Eye

my armpit.

"Sonnet, run home and tell Mama we got a deer. Papa and I need to track her. Go home now." But Sonnet would not let go of me. The bond between twins was strong and in a world where English was just becoming our second language, it was even stronger. Sonnet always looked up to me as her older brother, though she was older by one minute.

"Jost, let's go. Have your sister go on her way."

"Sonnet, go home."

"I hate Papa," she whispered in my ear. Then she parted and ran home.

"I never see her push meat away from the dinner table," Papa said.

"Papa, she's a girl."

"Come on, boy," he said, as he rubbed his hand on my head.

The deer only made it 30 yards before it ran out of air. She was a beautiful creature. Papa would normally kill bucks but it had been a while since we had meat to eat.

The year was 1931 and our arrival in the United States of America had occurred just two years prior. My father had worked in the shipyards of Stockholm, Sweden. The shipbuilding industry was hit hard during the Depression and work was nowhere to be found. Our family had considered other cities in Europe but most cities were worse

Jost: Coming to America

off than Stockholm.

So in 1929 we boarded a ship heading for New York to find a new life in America. Papa had an uncle in Virginia who had agreed to sponsor us.

The ship was the freighter named *Vulcan*. My father and another man had signed on with the ship for a one-way assignment in the maintenance and engineering department. We were forced to share a small cabin with the other man's family. They had two children; one was a baby and the other was a boy my age. He was a sickly child who may have been autistic. All day long he would sit in the corner of the small cabin and stare at his fingers which he moved with incredible speed. His expression was blank. His mother would just look at him and shake her head in disbelief. His sickliness also played tricks with his bowels which he could not control. Our little cabin, which was just large enough for two, was packed with eight, two of whom had toileting problems. The cabin smelled like shit and to make matters worse, none of us were allowed to leave the cabin. The 30-day crossing was as close to hell as I can remember. I recall asking Sonnet to kill me. She said she would do it, if I would kill her first.

Each day my father would return to the cabin with some bread, water and raw vegetables. This is what we lived on. Our diet combined with the smell of shit and the frequent seasickness robbed

In the Blink of an Eye

us of any fat we had. I could count the ribs on Sonnet's torso. Her beautiful face had turned ugly. I was so afraid to see how I looked that I refused to look in the mirror. Some nights Papa would go back to work and Sonnet and I would sit together in the corner of the cabin trying to make the best of our situation.

"Jost, tell me a story. Tell me a story about how life is going to be in America and promise me things will get better."

"Things will be wonderful in America. You and I are going to make many friends. We are going to live in a big house with beautiful gardens. Our house will be near the water like it was in Stockholm and we will learn how to sail. Mama will make you new dresses for school and you will be a great student. Someday you'll go to the University. I will be a great athlete and compete in the Olympics and will win a medal for America." And by the time the story was over, Sonnet was asleep.

During the last third of the trip the Atlantic turned ugly. The seas had built to 30 feet and a few times *Vulcan* rolled so hard to port or to starboard that everything in our cabin went airborne. We were all vomiting. The vomit was everywhere and the stench was so overwhelming that Sonnet passed out for a few moments. And while it was a time for hysterics, Mama stayed tough. She was a rock. She saw the bright side of everything. Even during

Jost: Coming to America

our hell she would say, "Look, I see the statue, I see the statue. She is waiting for us. The lady with the torch is waiting for Jost and Sonnet."

In the Blink of an Eye

Chapter 7

Jost:
Arrival in New York

Arrival in New York was wonderful and exciting. The morning of our arrival was the first time we were allowed out of our cabin. The air outside was cool and the fact that it didn't smell like the cabin was so delightful, it was hard to explain. There was a slight mist that made the detail of the harbor hard to distinguish. Then Mama said, "Look, children, there she is. There she is. We are here at last." Then I could see her.

"Where, Jost?"

"Just look beyond the other boats." Then Sonnet saw the lady and started to cry.

"Jost, no more cabin, no more ocean. We are

In the Blink of an Eye

home." Papa joined us at the rail.

"Children, we should be meeting Uncle tomorrow. We will need to stay on the ship tonight but if you want, you can sleep on deck."

"Fine with us," we said in unison.

That night we slept on the deck of the ship in the cool, damp New York City air. "I love America," I thought to myself. "I can't wait to meet Uncle," I said to Sonnet, but she was already asleep. The next morning, my father escorted us to a shower room where I had my first shower since leaving Sweden. This was also the first time I'd seen myself in the mirror. I was skin and bones. He walked in.

"Stop staring at yourself. Uncle will fatten you up."

Later that morning we met Uncle at the pier. He looked like my father, only older and more worn.

"Erick, how was the trip over?"

"A bit rough on the family. We need to get some food into these little bodies," Papa said as he stared down at us.

"Come on, we need to get to immigration."

We walked for about an hour before we came to the office that would grant us passage to our new country. The immigration officer was a big man whose hands were too big for any size body. Uncle filled in form after form while speaking to the officer. The four of us just sat quietly as none of us

Jost: Arrival in New York

were able to understand English. Then the officer took out a large stamp and pounded it into the forms. Each time the stamp hit the forms, the table vibrated. Then the officer handed him four forms, each with the appropriate stamp, and mumbled something to Uncle.

"What did he say, Uncle?"

"Welcome to America. Welcome to America."
"Sonnet, we are Americans now," I said.

"No Jost, not until I sleep in a proper American bed." We laughed.

The only thing now on my mind was food. "Mama, can we eat?"

"Yes, soon."

We walked for another hour through the maze of streets and people, until we arrived at the train station. Papa gave Uncle some money for our train tickets.

"Children, we don't leave for two hours so we can eat now." Uncle took the family to a small restaurant inside the terminal. I sat down and looked at the menu. Not a word of Swedish. Then Uncle exchanged a few words with the waitress and within a few minutes, we were served. Each plate was full of bacon, eggs and toast. Sonnet and I got milk. It was extra cold. I guzzled down the first glass. Then a second glass appeared. With each bite, Sonnet closed her eyes and chewed slowly.

"Sonnet, what are you doing?"

In the Blink of an Eye

"Jost, close your eyes and focus on the taste." So I did and I could see she was right. It was truly wonderful. When we were through, another plate of eggs and bacon came to the table, which Sonnet and I shared.

"Do you feel better now?" asked Uncle.

"Much better." We thanked Uncle and relished in how good it felt to not be hungry.

At 3 p.m. we boarded the train for Newport News, Virginia. The train had sleeper cars. Our compartment had four bunks. The adults had their own bunks while Sonnet and I shared the other. We slept at opposite ends and within minutes of lying down, we were fast asleep. The train made many stops but neither Sonnet nor I ever woke up until we reached Newport News. I remember so vividly walking off the train and into the terminal. There were so many African people. "Uncle, is America in Africa?"

"No, Jost. You have a lot to learn."

Sonnet simply looked at me and rolled her eyes.

The taxi ride to Uncle's home took about 25 minutes. Uncle lived in the county on a small farm. The farmhouse was small but nice. My aunt had died some years earlier so Uncle lived alone. There were cows and chickens and a pig that roamed the farmyard. There was also a big garden. The house had three bedrooms, one of which was for Sonnet and me to share. The Virginia heat was also something we were not used to, especially coming from Sweden.

That night at dinner, discussions started to focus on work for Papa and school for Sonnet and me.

"Yoseph, thank you so much for taking us in."

"Family has to look after family," Uncle replied.

"Tomorrow I'll take you to see a man I know at the boatyard in Hampton. He says he needs a good carpenter in the yard. And after that I will take Evon to school so the children can get registered."

Next door to Uncle's farm was another farming family. These people were dairy farmers. They had many children, several of which were my age. Within a few days they became our friends and were committed to teaching us English. For Sonnet the new language came easily, but for me it was more difficult. By the time school started, we could get by, but I would never earn a grade higher than a "C."

Our first year of life in Virginia slid by. We got used to the weather, the people and living with Uncle. My father's job at the boatyard was going well and on Sundays he and I would go to the yard to work on a special project. We were building a sailboat for Sonnet and me. The boat was a 19-foot daysailer. She had an open cockpit and a wooden mast that carried the mainsail. The tiller was long which made it easy to steer from any position. The boat was big enough for the family but not big enough for the seas that would often build in the Chesapeake Bay.

The summer of 1934 was a bad time. That was the year that Uncle died. He had contracted some type of disease that caused him to lose weight. He experienced terrible stomach pain and eventually stopped eating. After just a few months, he died at home in his bedroom. His death was particularly hard on Sonnet, who had grown very close to him. Uncle had left the farm to Papa. This took a tremendous financial burden off the shoulders of my parents.

Life on the farm seemed to stabilize. Mama and Sonnet tended to the garden while Papa and I tended to the few chickens and cows that roamed the yard. Papa also hunted regularly, which was something Sonnet didn't approve of. Our friendships at school continued to grow. Kids called me Pup, a nickname I didn't quite understand. Richard, one of the kids who lived next door, started the nickname because he said that the only other animal he'd ever seen that had one blue eye and one brown eye was a puppy he'd seen scavenging through a garbage can on Main Street. And while the name didn't bother me, I didn't like the stares

Jost: Arrival in New York

I would get from people who witnessed my oddity for the first time. Nevertheless, it was the name that stuck with me until the day I died.

In the Blink of an Eye

Chapter 8

Jost:
Adrift in the Bay

The daysailer Papa and I built was christened *Sea Pup*. We went with *Sea Pup* rather than *Sea Dog* because *Sea Pup* was small and young. In honor of my oddity, *Sea* was painted in blue and *Pup* painted in brown. The words stood out beautifully against the whitewashed transom. Sonnet loved to sail with me, but from time to time would complain about not having her own boat. Girls complain a lot. Sonnet was an excellent helmsman though she would always correct me and make me say helmsgirl. Like all boats, *Sea Pup* was a girl. This was another issue Sonnet loved to debate. She insisted *Sea Pup* was a boy. I referred to the boat as she and

In the Blink of an Eye

Sonnet referred to her as he. This issue was never settled as Papa agreed with me and Mama agreed with Sonnet. Life is full of stalemates, I learned later in life. We kept *Sea Pup* on Sunset Creek near the boatyard and near the beautiful stately homes that lined the shore. Papa made us sail mostly on the Hampton River and around the Roads, but never beyond Fort Wool. That was our understanding and it was also a commitment I intended to keep. It is also a commitment that was broken.

It was the early fall of 1936 and Sonnet and I were approaching our 16th birthday. We had planned to sail *Sea Pup* over to Fort Wool and then to Willoughby Bay or to the Elizabeth River. We packed lunch for ourselves and had taken an old pillowcase that we packed with a sweater and a hat for each of us. The day started out relatively warm and sunny for an October day. Unfortunately the weather didn't stay that way. At 10 a.m. we launched *Sea Pup*, raised her sails, and sailed away from the banks of Sunset Creek.

"Pup, where is the anchor?" I looked in the compartment that normally held the anchor. It was empty.

"We must have left it onshore when we launched her."

"You mean him."

"Whatever."

"Jost, let's go back and get it," Sonnet said in a

Jost: Adrift in the Bay

concerned voice.

"Don't worry, we'll be fine."

"Papa said never to leave without the anchor."

"Fine, Sonnet, go swim back to shore and get it."

"Sometimes I hate you, Jost." The discussion ended.

The purpose of the anchor was twofold. One was to secure the boat if you wanted to stop for lunch, go swimming or go fishing. The other was to stop the boat from drifting if the wind died and the current was pulling you away from shore. Papa always said to throw out the anchor and all the line and steer toward shore. Eventually the anchor would grab and hold you in place until the tide changed. Once the tide changed you could drift home with the incoming current.

As the day passed by, the weather began to change and the fog started to roll in. And with the fog, the winds died and the tide started to run out of Hampton Roads. We were dead in the middle of the Roads when I realized that we were being carried away from land and into the open waters of the Chesapeake Bay. "Sonnet, put on your sweater." She put it on and stared at me.

"Pup, you shouldn't have left without the anchor. Papa is going to kill us."

"Sonnet, we'll be okay," I said in a frustrated tone. "We'll be okay."

In the Blink of an Eye

The outgoing tide was running at 2 knots and would run for four hours. That meant we would be approximately eight miles away from shore. I wasn't worried about the distance but rather about the fishing boats that would be coming back to port. We had no lights and no horn on *Sea Pup*.

With the evening temperatures starting to drop, Sonnet started to shiver. "Come here." She moved next to me and I put my arm around her shoulder. "Try not to think about it."

"Jost, are we going to die out here in this stupid boat?"

"No. If the winds pick up we'll sail home and if they don't, we will have to wait for the tide to change. I have a compass. We'll make it home, I promise."

For the next hour we continued to drift farther and farther away from the safety of Sunset Creek. Sonnet started to doze in the darkness. "Sonnet, wake up. You have to help me look and listen for other boats." Then off in the distance I could hear the drone of an engine. Then there was a blast from the fog horn. But there was no light. The drone sound grew louder and louder. Then 20 yards away, I could see the wake of the fishing vessel moving at 6 knots. We both jumped up and started to yell, hoping to gain their attention, but they simply passed us by. They never saw us and thank God they didn't hit us.

Jost: Adrift in the Bay

Hour after hour we sat together shivering and wishing we were home and warm. At 10 p.m. the tide slowed and we stopped drifting. The wind was still and it felt like we were suspended in air. Then I felt a bump and then another bump. "Sonnet, I think we're aground."

"Jost, is that the shoreline?"

"I think so. I wonder if we are on the flats." I leaned over the boat and stuck my leg over the transom. "Sonnet, we're aground." I pulled out the centerboard, took off my pants, and hopped into two feet of water. "I'm going to drag you ashore." Twenty minutes later I pulled *Sea Pup* up to a tree and tied her to a limb that hung out over the shore. We walked ashore. "I think we must be in Grandview or Poquoson."

"Do you know, or are you guessing?" Sonnet asked.

"Guessing."

"What do we do now, Pup?"

"Wait for the tide to change or for some wind. Anyway, we can't do anything until morning."

"Papa is going to kill us."

"I know," I said in a voice of defeat.

Over the next eight hours we tried to sleep and tried to stay warm but all we could do was lie next to each other and shiver. The sand was damp from the fog that embraced the shore since midday. This type of weather also brought out the sand fleas

45

In the Blink of an Eye

which found great pleasure snacking on our young tender skin. All I could think about was whether this was worse than the time we had lain cramped in the cabin of *Vulcan*. No matter how hard I tried to find some comfort in being alive, I could not overcome the terrible feeling of constant shivering. My muscles were so exhausted that they started to cramp and once again I thought how wonderful it would be to be dead.

As the sun started to rise, I noticed the fog was gone and the winds were up. Sonnet was numb and speechless. "Sonnet, let's go, we need to sail home."

"Pup, are we dead?"

"No, I don't think so. Come on, get up." I helped her up and walked to *Sea Pup*. "Get in. Get ready to raise the main."

"Okay, Captain," she replied sarcastically. Then the sails filled the air. I hopped in and we were off. As we sailed away, I looked for some indication of our whereabouts. Then I saw a pier in the distance. "I think we had run aground in Grandview."

"I think you're right," Sonnet replied.

While we were fortunate to have winds of 8 knots, it was unfortunately on the nose. This meant the sail home required long tacks. The first tack took us to Ocean View. The seas were now building and while rough, we were making good progress.

Jost: Adrift in the Bay

"Do you think Papa will be looking for us?" asked Sonnet.

"I suspect so," I replied.

"He's going to kill us," Sonnet said again.

"Please stop saying that." Ninety minutes later, we tacked again. This tack pointed us toward Fort Wool.

The ever rising sun created the needed heat required to stop the shivering. It was certainly welcome. We continued on. Then all of a sudden, a large blast sounded behind me. Then a voice followed over a loudspeaker.

"*Sea Pup*, *Sea Pup*, this is the Harbor Police. Drop your sails." I turned around. There was a 25-foot police boat approaching us. On deck were two police officers and a very familiar face.

"Papa," Sonnet said with mixed emotions.

The police boat pulled alongside. One of the police officers tossed a line to me.

"Tie it off to the bow cleat, boy."

"Yes, sir." Then Papa's large hand reached down to *Sea Pup* and grabbed Sonnet by the arm. Then he spouted something in Swedish and embraced her. I looked at him and saw a tear rolling down his cheek. I'd never seen him cry before. Not even at Uncle's funeral.

"Who left the anchor on shore?" Papa asked.

"We did," Sonnet replied. That was Sonnet-speak for "twins stick together." Papa didn't buy it.

In the Blink of an Eye

Then the boat lurched forward. We were now in tow. I remained in *Sea Pup*. Papa said nothing. He simply stood facing forward with his arm around Sonnet. He knew I was responsible for leaving the anchor behind and was totally disappointed with my lack of judgment. There would be hell to pay when we returned to the farm.

Then my mind started to drift back to *Vulcan*. I remembered the hell we had to endure and wishing I was dead. "Maybe I should gently slip overboard and let myself drown. Death would be better than what lies ahead." Then I woke up from my daze. The smell of the boat's exhaust was overpowering "Death by asphyxiation," I thought. Papa looked back. His eyes were less filled with hate and anger than before. "Maybe I'll survive this," I thought.

By now an hour had passed. The police boat made its way down Sunset Creek and docked at the boatyard.

"Hope you learned your lesson," one police officer said.

"Yes, sir," I replied.

"Put the boat away," Papa said sternly.

"Yes, Papa." *Sea Pup* was led into her slip and tied down. Then Papa walked toward me.

"We have a lot to talk about when we get back to the farm."

"Yes, sir."

"Let's go home. Your poor mother has both of

you for dead."

"Papa, I'm so sorry."

"Hush, boy."

Ten minutes later we were at the farm. Mama came running to the car. She was crying. She approached us, put her arms around both of us and hugged us, for what seemed like an hour.

"Let's be thankful you're home and safe." And just like that, Mama had forgiven me. This was not the case for Papa.

In the Blink of an Eye

Chapter 9

Jost:
Breezehound is Born

Punishment comes in many flavors, but in the end, the flavors really come down to two. There is physical punishment and mental punishment. Physical punishment can hurt severely but rarely lasts long. Mental punishment is more akin to torture. It lasts longer with no end defined. Papa chose mental punishment. He decided to ban me from the use of *Sea Pup*. The only thing worse would be to have taken Sonnet or Mama away from me, which in some ways he did. For the next month he spent Sundays sailing with Sonnet while I was forced to stay on the farm and work.

One fall night as I lay in bed, Sonnet knocked

on my door and walked in.

"Jost, are you awake?"

"Yes, come in." She sat on the edge of my bed. "I want you to know our punishment is almost over."

"What do you mean our punishment? You are not being punished."

"Papa is punishing me by making me sail with him and not with you. We sail, but he says nothing."

"How do you know the punishment is about to end?"

"As we returned to the marina today I heard him mutter, 'Enough is enough.'"

"Sonnet, I hope you're right."

December was approaching and *Sea Pup* was now put away for the year. Papa had finally put the sailing incident behind him and things were back to normal. With Christmas around the corner, things at school and at the boatyard started to slow down. Mama was focused on baking and decorating the house, while Sonnet and I were making Christmas gifts for Mama and Papa. Sonnet had taken up knitting and sewing and had made beautiful hats and scarves for the whole family. I had purchased a used jewelry box that I was refinishing for Mama. For Papa, I was making a leather tool belt.

I bought an old leather vest from a local cob-

Jost: *Breezehound* is Born

bler. The vest had a rip in it which could not be repaired. Sonnet and I cut the vest into the needed pieces to make the tool belt. Then with help from Mama, I hand-sewed all of the pieces together. When completed, the tool belt would hold a hammer, two screwdrivers, two pliers and other assorted small tools. Both Sonnet and I were very proud of our gifts.

On Christmas morning we gathered around the tree. Mama had made tea and a special Swedish Christmas cake. Most years there was very little under the tree. This year was different. Under the tree was a large bag. It looked out of place. The tag read, "For *Sea Pup*."

"Children, this gift will be opened last," announced Papa. Sonnet and I rushed to open the other gifts. There were new sweaters for both of us. Sonnet also got a necklace that had belonged to Mama's mother. And I got a watch that Papa had gotten from the man whose boat Papa repaired.

Then Papa and Mama opened their gifts. First they opened Sonnet's, which they loved, and then they opened mine. Mama opened her package slowly, revealing the jewelry box.

"Jost, this is beautiful. Erick, look how beautiful this is."

"Jost, you did a great job on this," he said with a mixture of Swedish and broken English. Then he opened up his gift.

In the Blink of an Eye

"My God, Son. This is perfect. This is the finest tool belt I have ever seen."

"Mama and Sonnet helped me with the sewing." He stood up and placed the belt around his waist.

"The men at work will be very jealous when they see this." Then he leaned over and hugged us with a warmth and love I had forgotten he had.

"Now, children, it's time for the last gift. Sit on the sofa." He reached over and dragged the bag across the floor. "Go ahead, open it." Sonnet and I opened the bag and looked inside. I could see a grommet on the cloth.

"Papa, what is it?" Sonnet said in a voice of confusion.

"Well, first, there are two things in the bag, not one. You must share them." By now I was pulling the fabric out of the bag.

"Papa, are these new sails for *Sea Pup*?"

"Better than that. These are two racing sails."

"Racing sails?" Sonnet said, still confused. "*Sea Pup* is not a racer. She's a daysailer."

"Not any more. She is being modified for racing at the yard. And these are her new racing sails. You have been day-sailing long enough. It's time you start to race."

"Papa, girls don't race."

"Then you will be the exception, Sonnet. There's going to be a big race this summer for children under 18. I want you to enter and I want you to win."

"Papa, this is wonderful," Sonnet said with an uncontrollable excitement. "Jost, this is great news. We can sail together again."

"Maybe it's time for a new name. *Sea Pup* is not fitting for a race boat," I said.

"Papa, how about *Breezehound*?"

"I like that, Sonnet," I said with confidence and acceptance.

"Then *Breezehound* it is. *Breeze* will be in blue and *hound* will be in brown, in honor of the colors of *Sea Pup*, my brother and her captain."

"Done," Papa exclaimed.

In the Blink of an Eye

Chapter 10

Jost:
Off to the Races

By April, *Sea Pup* had been transformed to *Breeze-hound*. She was fitted with a deeper centerboard. Her mast was moved aft by three feet and her boom had been shortened. A forestay was added to accommodate the new racing jib. Winches were added to each side of the cockpit and a shorter rudder handle was installed. Papa believed that *Breeze-hound* would be very competitive, if the helmsman and the trimmer could sharpen their skills.

Papa had the new name painted on the transom. He also had a picture of a greyhound painted on the bow. Greyhounds are the fastest dog on earth and Papa intended *Breezehound* to be the fast-

In the Blink of an Eye

est boat on the Chesapeake Bay. According to Sonnet, *Breezehound* was more beautiful than *Sea Pup*. When I looked at her I didn't see beauty, I saw raw racing energy, the kind hunting dogs have when they chase down their prey. *Breezehound* seemed to growl like a dog ready to bite. She was hungry for the sea and hungry for a race.

Shortly after *Breezehound* was launched, Papa purchased a racing skills book for Sonnet and me. This presented a few problems as Papa wasn't able to read the book or explain the technical aspects of racing to us. Sonnet, who was the best with English, took it upon herself to read the book, and taught us what the text was saying. She was an excellent teacher and within weeks we had mastered all of the technical language associated with racing. This technical understanding caused Papa and me to make a few more adjustments to *Breezehound*.

As spring continued its path toward summer, racing lessons began. Papa had a co-worker, Mr. Geary, whose son had won many races in the juniors division. Each Saturday regardless of the weather, Sonnet, Tim and I practiced. Tim taught us everything about the importance of the start, how to run the line, how to properly tack, gibe, reach and run. We learned about shifting weight, how to adjust the sails and all the rules of racing. Tim had established a race course in and around the Hampton River and Willoughby Bay. He would pace us with his small motorboat and time us with his stopwatch. Within weeks our times had improved and Sonnet and I started to believe that we could actually win a race.

The big race was called the Hampton Skippers race. It would be run in mid-July just before the light winds of August would be upon us. In preparation for this, Papa had enrolled us in the junior racing series, a twice a week race for juniors that took place just outside the Hampton River. Most kids who raced were from families that belonged to the local yacht club. We were too poor for membership to the club, and for that reason alone, were the most motivated to win. Despite our poverty, *Breezehound* was as good a boat as any in the fleet. And now that she had been refined and re-refined, she was poised to win.

The race series began in the first week of June. The advantage we had over the other boats was Sonnet. First, she was the only girl in the fleet of helmsmen and trimmers, and that alone was a huge intimidation factor for the all-male crews. Second, because she was so small, she also gave us a weight advantage. Yes, Sonnet may have proved to be my secret weapon.

The first race took place in perfect conditions. The wind blew at 10 knots, in fairly flat seas. There were 15 boats in the fleet, each one meeting a certain set of guidelines that eliminated the need for

In the Blink of an Eye

handicaps. Five minutes before the start, we positioned *Breezehound* to attack the start line on a starboard tack. This meant the boats on a port tack would have to yield to us. As the clock ticked down, we came about and started our run to the line. Five of the 15 boats followed us and were less than a boat length behind. The other boats were on a port tack, a decision they would live to regret.

When the horn blew, we were in perfect position and crossed the starting line first. "Sonnet, trim the jib. Quick!"

"Trimming," she replied.

"Now move to the rail." Sonnet moved to windward and put herself on the windward rail. *Breezehound* dug in. We had the lead but were being challenged by the four other boats that were just behind us at the start.

"Pup, you have a boat starting to overcome us. Trim the main."

"It's fine, Sonnet."

"Shift your weight."

"I'm trying."

By the time our verbal exchange was over, we were in second place, but only behind by a half-boat length. Then I felt the air pick up. The other boats started to round up. I released the tension on the main and regained the lead. The race toward the first marker was a battle of equals, with *Breezehound* exchanging the lead three times with two other boats. When we turned the first mark, we were in second place, but only by one boat length.

The race toward the second marker was downwind. Weight is a very important factor in downwind sailing and this is when Sonnet's small size would really pay off. The downwind leg was approximately two miles long. Some of the skippers set their sails for a broad reach and some set them wing and wing. We chose the broad reach which forced us to sail a bit off the rhumb line. Inch by inch, we pulled away from the other boats. Sonnet's small size was helping. Several other boats followed us but no one could keep up. Halfway through the leg we were six boat lengths ahead of the next boat. The second half of the downwind leg favored us yet again as the wind shifted, allowing us to move more directly in line with the marker.

The marker was now two yards away and we were clearly in the lead. At the turn we were still six boat lengths ahead of the second-place boat. The distance between the second-place boat and the rest of the fleet was imperceptible. The next leg was sailed with the wind 90° to our boat. Sonnet moved to the windward side using what little weight she had to help stabilize the boat. The fleet was gaining on us and the view from the stern was like watching a pack of wolves chasing the deer. Eight boats were fighting for second place and each one had their eye on *Breezehound*.

In the Blink of an Eye

As we turned the final marker, we maintained our lead, but had lost some of the advantage we had over the other boats. The fleet was now separated, with three of the eight boats just two lengths behind us. The battle continued. We would need to make one final maneuver before we crossed the finish line. This was when tactics would play a major factor in the outcome.

"Pup, let's tack."

"No, not yet. I think we should still go another 25 yards. Sonnet, get ready to shift your weight."

"Okay, ready."

"Ready. Let's go." The tack was executed perfectly. The other boats started to mimic our move. One by one they tacked, and one by one, they started to gain on us.

"Pup, bring her up."

"Got it."

"Come on, hang in there," Sonnet said nervously. Then we heard the sound of the horn, indicating we were first to cross the finish line. We had won by one-half boat length.

"Pup, we did it. We did it!"

I looked over to the shore to see Papa and Mama with their arms raised overhead. Yes, we won the first race of the season. What a sweet triumph for two kids who didn't belong to the yacht club and what a triumph for Papa, the designer and builder of *Breezehound*.

Chapter 11

The Yacht Club

The phone rang six times before someone from Mick Dermott's office answered it.

"Edward Dermott's office."

"Good morning. This is Michael Kenney. Is Mick Dermott in?"

"Yes, let me get him."

It had been several weeks since I talked to Mick Dermott and quite frankly, I had not yet gotten back to thinking clearly since I got the news of my inheritance.

"Mickey Dermott."

"Hey, Mick Dermott, Michael."

"Michael, how are you? I hear you moved out of the Sterns' house."

In the Blink of an Eye

"Yes, I got an apartment on Queen Street, in the building where the sail loft is located."

"Very modest for a millionaire."

"I know. I'm not sure where my life is heading and besides, I like the smell of Dacron in the morning." We both laughed.

"So Michael, what can I do for you?"

"I want to meet for lunch."

"Okay. When and why?"

"When is this week. And why, I want you to do some research for me."

"Research on what?"

"It's not what. It's who."

"Okay then, who?"

"I'll explain that over lunch."

"Okay, let's meet at the yacht club on Thursday at noon."

"Fine. See you then."

"Great."

The apartment was perfect. Despite its small size, it had charm and character. It was downtown and that's where I wanted to be. It did have one shortcoming, however. No ceiling fans. That could be easily remedied. Later that day, I had purchased two ceiling fans; one for the living room to create a breeze, and the other for my bedroom and for my addiction. Then I drove to East Mellen Street to browse the antique/ junk shops. When I came to the junkiest one, I walked inside.

"How can we help you?"

The Yacht Club

"I'm looking for a TV; the older, the better."

"I have one black-and-white set. It's not cable-ready and has a cracked case."

"Fine, how much?"

"Five dollars."

"I'll take it."

"Do you want to try it first?"

"Sure. Okay, plug it in." He brought out the TV, plugged it in and then turned it on. He adjusted the rabbit ears but there was nothing but snow.

"Sorry I can't get a picture."

"No problem; it's perfect." I handed him five dollars and walked out of the store with my other addiction toy.

By Thursday, I could hardly deal with the stress associated with my lunch with Mick Dermott. I walked to the yacht club from my apartment. With every step I got closer to staring my preincarnation in the face. This meeting, I hoped, would prove to me once and for all where my soul resided prior to my birth.

The wind was unusually still and the sea smell from the Hampton River infiltrated what air there was to breathe. As I approached the yacht club, I noticed that Mick Dermott's car was missing. I glanced at my watch and noticed that it had taken only seven minutes to walk over. I had allotted 30 minutes. The yacht club was somewhere I rarely went and never entered by myself. I was not a member, but I was a multimillionaire. So as awkward as it felt, I opened the door and walked in as if I owned the place. The restaurant was empty except for the bartender who was busy straightening

In the Blink of an Eye

up the bar. He was a man in his early 60s whose face, arms and hands were weathered in a way that made him look like someone who had spent his life in the elements. He walked with a slight limp, his hair was gray and cut close to his head. I walked to the bar.

"Here for lunch?" he said with a New England accent.

"Yes, I'm meeting someone at noon."

"You're a bit early."

"Yes, I know."

"Well, pick a table or you can wait at the bar." I sat down and ordered an iced tea.

"Are you local?" the bartender asked.

"Yes, I live on Queen Street."

The bartender extended his hand. "Jackie Vee."

"Nice to meet you. I'm Michael Kenney."

"By any chance are you related in any way to Stephen Kenney?"

"Yes, I'm his son."

"My god, I heard he had a boy. That was a terrible accident. Sorry for your mom and dad's death."

"Yeah, thanks. Did you know him?"

"Oh, yes. You know he was a terrific sailor. He won more races than any other, back then. People used to call us the Triple Crown Boys."

"Why's that?"

"Your dad and I and another guy all raced against each other. Between the three of us, we won all of the races in the racing seasons. Your dad was about half the age of me and the other guy. He was in his 20s and we were in our 40s."

The Yacht Club

"What was the other guy's name?"

"I don't know his proper name. Everyone just called him Pup. Pup Alexson, I think."

Instantly, beads of sweat formed all over me. I could feel them running down my back and I went numb.

"Are you okay? You look like you're ready to faint." The room was spinning. The feeling of anxiety came over me.

"I said, are you all right, Michael?" I didn't answer. Instead, I picked up the iced tea glass and pressed it against my head. My consciousness returned and the room stopped spinning.

"You did say Pup Alexson."

"Yep, that's what I said."

"What do you remember about him?"

"He had a sister that raced with him from time to time, and he had weird eyes."

"What about his eyes?"

"One was blue and one was brown. He looked freakish."

"Anything else?"

"Yeah, his voice was like yours. In fact, if you had that eye thing he had, it would be like he was standing here in front of me."

"Glad I wore my colored contact lens," I thought to myself. "Do you know what happened to him and his sister?"

"Pup died back in the early '60s, and his sister, I have no idea."

"How did he die?"

In the Blink of an Eye

"Car accident; but it really didn't matter."

"Why's that?" I asked.

"He also had a brain tumor. The tumor gave him memory problems. Maybe he forgot where he was going. I kind of miss the old guy." Jackie shook his head.

"Does the yacht club keep any archives from the '60s?"

"Yeah, all the racing plaques are kept upstairs. If you go up there, you'll find many with the Triple Crown Boys' names inscribed."

At that moment, Mick Dermott walked in.

"Hey, Jackie."

"Hey, Mickey."

"How are you doing, Michael?"

"Great. Good to see you, Mick Dermott."

"Looks like you guys are in a deep discussion."

"We're just getting acquainted," I said, trying to keep Mick Dermott away from our discussion.

"Well, Michael, ready for lunch?"

"Sure." We left the bar and walked over to a table that overlooked the endless collection of sailboats.

"This is really a neat place," I said.

"I know. You should think about becoming a member. Your father was a member here for years."

"So I just found out."

We ordered lunch and engaged in general conversation, mostly about what I was doing now that I had money in my pockets. I mentioned doing some volunteer work for the local food bank and a disaster relief organization. Then lunch arrived and we started to eat

The Yacht Club

our crab cakes.

"So, Michael, you called this meeting. What's on your mind?"

"Mick Dermott, I want to hire you to do some research for me."

"I know. What do you want me to research?"

"As I mentioned it is not what, it is who."

"Okay, who?"

"I want you to find out everything you can about a guy named Jost (Pup) Alexson and his sister. I think her name was Sonnet."

"Sonnet, like the car you drive?"

"Yeah, I know it's weird. I don't know if she ever got married. Jost died about 20 years ago, according to Jackie Vee. He was probably born in the '20s and came here from Europe. He lived in the area until he died."

"Why are you so interested in this guy and his sister?"

"I understand he raced with my father and I want to learn about the people in my father's life." I couldn't believe I was lying to Mick Dermott. "I also want you to find out anything you can about Audrey Alying."

"The girl you dated in college?"

"Yeah, that's the one."

"Okay, at least that I understand. Give me two to three weeks. Is that okay?"

"That's fine."

"By the way, nice contact lenses."

"Thanks. I bought one blue set and one brown set. It was the first thing I bought after I got my inheri-

In the Blink of an Eye

tance."

"To each his own."

Soon after lunch was finished, the bill came.

"Charge it to my account."

"Sure thing, Mick."

"Come on, Michael, I'll drive you back to Queen Street."

"Go ahead. I'm going to hang out here for awhile."

"Okay. I'll call you as soon as I have something."

"Great."

After Mick Dermott left, I went to the second floor and started to look at all the plaques that were hung on the walls.

1957—First Place-Stephen Kenney.
Second Place-Pup Alexson (me).
Third Place-Jackie Vee.

1958—First Place-Pup Alexson.
Second Place-Stephen Kenney.
Third Place-Jackie Vee.
    "I beat my father that year."

1959—First Place-Stephen Kenney.
Second Place-Pup Alexson.
Third Place-Jackie Vee.

1960—First Place-Pup Alexson.
Second Place-Stephen Kenney.
Third Place-Jackie Vee.
    "I beat him again."

The Yacht Club

1961—*In memory of Pup Alexson*
First Place-Stephen Kenney.
Second Place-Jackie Vee.
Third Place-James Dugan.

1962—First Place-Stephen Kenney.
Second Place-Jackie Vee.
Third Place-James Dugan.

1963 – *In memory of Stephen Kenney*
First Place-Jackie Vee.
Second Place-Keith Schlueter.
Third Place-Ricky Feldman.

In the Blink of an Eye

Chapter 12

Face to Face

The drive to Washington, D.C., seemed to take forever and given my recent prosperity, I should've rented a car with air-conditioning. But instead I drove the old Saab two-seater. I drove in silence, a ritual I practiced more often than not. My hotel room was next to the temple; very convenient, considering how long I was planning on staying.

"Hello, how can I help you?"

"My name is Michael Kenney. I have a reservation."

"Yes, Mr. Kenney. I have your reservation and paperwork ready for you. You will be with us for two weeks. Is that correct?"

In the Blink of an Eye

"Yes."

"I have you in a king bed, non-smoking. I see you have requested a room with a ceiling fan."

"Yes, that's right."

"Okay. We can accommodate that."

"Great."

"Room 1210. The elevators are just down the hall."

"Thanks. Room 1210, nice number, my birthday."

The room was fairly basic, but nice. The windows provided a view of the temple, a few restaurants, and several homeless people. It was now time to think about what my next move was to be. What if Mick Dermott was able to find Audrey or Sonnet? Would I attempt to make contact with them? I clicked on the ceiling fan, lay down on the bed and started to blink. I was back at Houghton Plantation. Angel Lehcar appeared in the slivers of darkness. Her hands reached out to me like a toddler reaches out to be picked up by her mother. I can hear my own voice. "Angel, what do you want? Why do you keep putting your arms out to me?" Then I hear a shot. "What was that? Was that from the flash or outside?" I ran to the window but there was no change in the scene outside. I went back to bed. Flash after flash, I saw Angel staring at me with her arms extended. Her mouth was moving, but I could hear nothing. Then I fell asleep.

Face to Face

"Michael, Michael." It was Audrey's voice. "I know about you and your addiction. Why did you push me away?"

I forced myself awake and realized it was morning. "Twelve hours lost to exhaustion," I thought.

By 10 a.m. I had performed my ablutions and was standing at the entrance to the temple. I was planning on spending a few weeks with the monks, specifically trying to understand the power and the wisdom of the Buddha. Jodii, one of the monks who I had befriended, was in his late 20s, which made him my elder by a few dozen months. He had studied in India under the guardianship of his Holiness. He and I had talked frequently over the last two years and I considered him my spiritual mentor. We sat in a small meditation room.

"Jodii, I continue to have visions of my preincarnations. I understand who I was and my existence has been confirmed. I have unsettled feelings for a certain woman whom I both love and fear. I have lost her and I want her back."

"Michael, you have suffered too much. You should seek love and joy. Remember, your heart will be filled with love and peace when, and only when, wisdom and compassion become the basis for your life. You need to spend time in meditation until you realize the essence of the balance between your past suffering and your future joy. Let's meditate together."

In the Blink of an Eye

The sound of the chants and the smell of the incense allowed me to slide into the meditative state that I needed so badly. Several hours later I awoke to a clear head and a clear heart. I was demon free, but not free of Audrey. On the last day of my visit, Jodii presented me with a large bag of sand.

"Michael, this is sacred sand, blessed by his Holiness. Take the sand and spread it about the world. Use it as healing power. Do good in the world and find your love."

"Thank you, old friend. Here, this is for the monastery." Inside the envelope was a check for $15,000. It was money well spent.

On the second day following my return to Queen Street, I heard from Mick Dermott.

"Michael, how are you? I have the info you're looking for. Are you free for lunch?"

"Sure."

"Noon at the yacht club?

"Okay, see you there." At 11:30 a.m. I put in my brown contact lenses and started to walk to the club.

"Michael, wait up." I turned around to see Mick Dermott walking behind me.

"So Mick Dermott feels like a little exercise?"

"Yeah, I'm trying to keep this old body in shape."

"So what's in the envelope?"

"The info you wanted."

Face to Face

"Did you find Audrey?"

"Not exactly."

"What do you mean, not exactly?"

"Let's talk over lunch."

"I guess I can wait."

The parking lot of the yacht club was empty. We walked inside.

"Hey, Mickey."

"Hi, Jackie."

"Michael, where have you been?" asked Jackie Vee.

"I was in Northern Virginia visiting friends."

"You really remind me of that guy Pup. Actually, you look more like him than your father."

"Go figure," I replied.

We took a table in the corner, sat down and ordered two beverages and two crabcake platters.

"Okay, Mick Dermott. What did you find?"

"Who do you want to start with?"

"Audrey."

"Fine." He pulled out a letter from the government and slid it over to me.

"Audrey purchased a passport a few months ago. She also purchased an airline ticket to Puerto Rico. We found no address in the U.S. and her driver's license was renewed in San Juan. We were unable to locate her at the address that was provided on the driver's license. We don't know anything beyond that, except her father died around the time she left for the Caribbean."

The crabcakes arrived and we started to eat.

"Jost Alexson died on December 10, 1960, in a car collision. Jost was buried in a cemetery in Phoebus, near East Mellen Street. I have his obituary and an article that appeared in the newspaper about the auto accident. He has one surviving relative."

"Did you say has, or had?"

"Has."

"Who?"

"Her name is Sonnet Alexson. She lives here in Hampton."

"You're kidding, right?"

"No. She lives in a senior housing development on Executive Drive. I think it is an assisted living facility. One more thing, Michael."

"What?"

"One of the people who died in the collision with Jost was a guy named Richard Brown."

"Who is he?"

"I believe he was the son of your grandparents' housekeeper."

"Really? See what you can find out about Richard Brown."

"Fine, but why do you want to know all this stuff?"

"What does it matter? I am your client. Why do you have to know?"

Face to Face

"I have been looking after you since your birth and I guess I can't let go."

"So, Mick Dermott, do you know why I want to know all this information?"

He hesitated, then pulled out a stack of newspaper articles from the 1940s to the 1960s that he borrowed from the club archives. He sorted through them and then extracted one from 1945 and slid it in front of me.

"Is this what it's all about?" I couldn't believe my eyes. Staring back at me was a picture of Pup Alexson at age 25. He just won a major race and was featured in the newspaper article. I felt like I was staring at myself. I started to sweat and a feeling of dizziness come over me.

"Michael, Michael." I felt Mick Dermott's hand grab my shoulders. "Don't pass out on me."

In the Blink of an Eye

Chapter 13

Blind Man's Bluff

For the next two weeks I stayed inside my apartment growing a beard and mustache. I needed to have a disguise if I was going to visit Sonnet Alexson. It was bad enough I shared his voice; I didn't need to share his looks too, if I could help it. A two-week prisoner in a two-bedroom apartment can be mind-numbing if you have nothing to do. That was not the case for me. Each day I spent hour upon hour on my bed staring up at the ceiling fan, blinking and seeing. One image flash was of Audrey and for a second I began to wonder if my flashes would start revealing my future rather than my past. In that single image Audrey was standing

In the Blink of an Eye

in front of a small house that had been destroyed by some type of natural force. Other than that one image of Audrey, the rest were of Jost, Sonnet and Angel. Some flashes were repeats and some were not. I felt like I was watching an old 8mm movie, one frame at a time. Angel continued to call out to me, her arms extended. At night, I tried to sleep but as usual, I was unsuccessful. The only thing I was achieving was exhaustion. On Day 10 of my two-week isolation I finally fell asleep. The sounds were repetitive. Angel's voice screaming, "Michael, Michael, Michael." There were the sounds of whips cracking, guns being fired, people moaning and the eerie sound of a door opening and closing. And then there was the voice of a man screaming "demon child." I would force myself awake only to remember Audrey's last words: "Don't let the demon get you, Angel." By now I knew all about Angel and all about the people that touched her life, from the beginning to the end. My understanding of Angel's life was complete.

The assisted living center was only five miles from my apartment. Based on what I knew, Sonnet was born in 1920. That would make her 64 years old. I wondered why someone so young would be living in an assisted living facility. The girl at the reception desk was busy doing paperwork when I walked in.

"Good morning, how can I help you?"

Blind Man's Bluff

"My name is Michael Kenney. I am a local writer and am compiling information for a new book about people who emigrated from Scandinavia in the early 1920s. I was wondering if Sonnet Alexson would be available to talk to me."

"Let me walk down to her apartment and see if she's available."

Some apartment, I thought. It's more like a modern college dormitory. Five minutes later, the girl returned.

"She'll meet with you in the social room."

"Great."

"Have a seat in the lobby, Mr. Kenney."

"Thanks." Ten minutes later a staff member walked into the lobby.

"Mr. Kenney, Ms. Alexson is in the social room."

"Great." I was so nervous, partly because I was about to see Sonnet but also because I was lying about being a local writer.

The room looked like a typical recreation room you expect to see in an assisted living facility. There were a lot of tables and chairs. People were sitting around watching TV, playing cards, reading and chatting. Sonnet sat in a corner in a high-back chair. She was facing the entrance. She looked very familiar. In fact, she was a carbon copy of the girl in my flashes, except for the nearly 50 years that had lapsed since she and Pup won their first

In the Blink of an Eye

race with *Breezehound*.

As I walked toward her, she stared at me. Her stare went through me as if I wasn't there. She had long brown hair that was pulled back in a ponytail. She was dressed in a white linen skirt and blouse. They reminded me of hippie clothing from the 1970s. I continued to walk toward her.

"Ms. Alexson?"

"Yes."

"I'm Michael Kenney." I extended my hand. There was a short hesitation from her and then she extended her hand. Our hands missed by two feet. I moved my hand toward hers until we touched. Then she grabbed it. Her skin was soft but her grip was hard.

"I'm sorry, Ms. Alexson."

"Nothing to be sorry about, Mr. Kenney."

"Call me Michael."

"Very well, Michael. Take me to the courtyard where we can have some quiet and where we can breathe some fresh air." I helped her out of her chair, grabbed her arm and walked her outside. "Let's sit by the flowers."

"Sure." We sat on the bench, both angled toward each other.

"Michael, it's remarkable how much you sound like my brother. So how can I help you?"

"First tell me about how you lost your vision."

"Back in 1960, it was December 9th I believe,

my brother and I were involved in a terrible car accident. The roads were icy, and the car he was driving was hit by another car, starting a chain reaction and multi-car pileup. Pup, my brother, was killed almost instantly. He was pronounced dead just after midnight. I suffered a head injury. When I awoke from the coma, I was blind, Pup was gone, and all I had was a message from a nurse who said that Pup would see me again."

"Was there anybody else killed or injured in the crash?"

"Yes, there were many but I don't know any specifics. So back to why you want to see me, Pup. I mean, Michael."

"I'm writing a book about people who emigrated to the U.S. from Europe and settled in Hampton Roads.

"How did you select me?"

"It was a recommendation from a guy named Jackie Vee, from the yacht club.

"Jackie Vee. I haven't seen him or heard from him since the accident." She chuckled.

"So Sonnet, tell me about your journey to America, and tell me about Jost."

"Jost, I haven't thought of him as Jost for so long. Everyone called him Pup."

"Why Pup?"

"One of the neighbor's kids called him that because he had one blue eye and one brown. The boy said he'd never seen anything or anyone like that, except for a puppy he once saw scavenging through a garbage can on Main Street."

"Story confirmed," I thought to myself. Then Sonnet started to tell me in great detail about all the events in her life, none of which were a surprise to me. She stopped, however, just before the end of the Skipper's Race.

"So what happened, who won?"

"Michael, I'm tired. Let's save that for another day. If I tell you everything, you won't come back. And you know, I don't get many visitors. I'm all alone. Call for an assistant so she can walk me back to my apartment."

"Sure." A few minutes later, the nurse arrived.

"Miss Sonnet, are you ready for your nap now?"

"Yes, but give me one more minute alone with Mr. Kenney," she said to the nurse. "Michael, when I was a little girl, I was quite a crybaby. I depended on my twin brother for emotional support. Whenever something was wrong, I would run to Jost and cry on his shoulder. He would always complain that I cried so much that my tears saturated his shirt and made his shoulder wet. But you probably knew that."

I was speechless. She winked at me as if she could see and then started to walk toward the nurse.

Blind Man's Bluff

"Come see me tomorrow."

"Okay, I will."

Five minutes later I was back in my Saab feeling totally drained. "But you probably knew that." Was she on to me, like Audrey was? I glanced into the rearview mirror and popped out the brown contact lens. "I guess I could shave off my beard and mustache," I thought to myself.

Over the next several days I sat with Sonnet in the courtyard among the flowers as she revealed more and more about her life and the life of Jost. She and Jost had won the Skipper's Race and many more after that. She covered the death of her parents, the life of Jost, his jobs in the boatyard and the girls he dated. I found myself getting quite emotionally attached to Sonnet, and why not? She was my sister in a weird sort of way. Each day that went by, she also seemed more attached to me as well. Then on the last day of our scheduled discussion, she hit me between the eyes.

"Michael, it's time that I am open and honest with you." Panic started to set in. "While I am blind and see nothing, I do have eyes. They are the eyes of all the people who work here; the nurses, the residents and the staff. They look out for me. I've been here for a long time. They are my family."

"Sonnet, where are you going with this?"

"I have been doing my own investigative work,

In the Blink of an Eye

and this is what I know. First, you are not a writer. You have not taken a single note since you came to visit me. You are the son of Stephen Kenney, Pup's racing competitor. That was confirmed by Jackie Vee. The first day you came to see me, you had a beard and mustache and now you are clean-shaven. You have Pup's eyes. I'm assuming the brown and blue are your real colors. In my apartment are many pictures of me and my brother. My nurse tells me that you look exactly like my brother did when he was in his 20s. My nurse says my brother has returned. You live near a sail loft. I can smell Dacron when you get near me. You drive a Saab Sonett. My father loved that car. Should I stop Mr. Kenney, or Pup, or whoever the hell you are?" Her voice sounded like that of a prosecuting attorney. I was speechless. "Are you going to say something or are you going to let an old lady die from curiosity?"

"Sonnet, I'm so sorry. Let me start from the beginning." And so I began my story of a sad but also joyous life; a life of images and dream sounds. I told her about the shack and Audrey, about the Bujew, and about all the details I had seen in the flashes. Sonnet listened, saying very little. I noticed that my detailed understanding of Jost was confirmed by her nodding.

"Sonnet, let me ask you something. When you told me about your crying on Jost's shoulder, you said I 'probably knew that' already. Why did you say that?"

"Michael, the moment I met you and shook your hand, I felt Pup's presence. It was a new feeling for me and when I realized that you were not taking notes, I knew that everything I was saying you had heard or witnessed before. I have been trying to understand why this has happened, but I cannot. But I'm glad it has and that you are here with me."

"I can't explain it either. Sonnet, there is one thing that Jackie Vee said to me that you have not mentioned."

"What's that?"

"Jackie mentioned that Jost had a brain tumor that affected his memory, and that the accident may have been linked to the tumor."

"The tumor was present but dormant. We all get forgetful in old age."

"Sonnet, 40 is not old."

"Yes I know, but I still think the tumor had nothing to do with the accident. So tell me more about Audrey."

"There's nothing more to tell."

"Somehow I feel she will be part of your future."

"That would be nice," I said.

"You will hear from her soon. I can feel it."

In the Blink of an Eye

Chapter 14

Sailing Again

The phone rang four times before I answered it. It was Su. I knew why she was calling. My mail must have been piling up. It was a reminder that I needed to complete my departure from the Sterns.

"Hi, Mom."

"How are you, Dear?"

"Great."

"How was your trip to the temple?"

" Fantastic. Jodii sends his regards."

"Mickey is coming over for dinner tomorrow. Come over and join us."

"Okay, what time?"

"Six o'clock."

In the Blink of an Eye

"Okay. How's Dad?"

"Good. He misses having you around."

"I know, I miss him too."

"Maybe you can go sailing together over the weekend?"

"I would like that. I'll see you tomorrow."

"I'll make your favorite, Michael."

"Rum and Coke?"

"No, pot roast." We laughed.

Thursday was another beautiful day. With no plans other than dinner I decided to go for sail. I didn't like sailing alone as I liked the social aspect of sailing. At my young age I knew very few people who were free like me. After searching deep and hard I came up with only one name.

"Hello, Sonnet. It's Michael."

"How are you?"

"Great. And you?"

"Not bad for an old, blind gal. Are you coming by to see me today?"

"No, I want to take you out."

" Really, where?"

"How about a short daysail?"

"Michael, I haven't been on a boat in 20 years."

"Would you feel better if I got a nurse to come along?" "No, I trust you. I'll do it."

"Perfect, I'll be over at 10 a.m."

Sonnet was ready when I arrived. She was

Sailing Again

dressed in blue jeans and a white collared golf shirt. She wore boat shoes and looked like she was ready to go. We drove to the marina, saying very little to each other until Sonnet spoke up.

"Michael, I'm so excited. I was thinking about asking you to take me, ever since you told me about your boat. I don't think I will be much help."

"We'll see."

When we arrived at the marina we walked to the boat. Sonnet walked beside me as if she had done it every day.

"Feels like a nice breeze, Michael."

"It feels like 8 knots. Here, let me help you." I got in the boat and prepared to take Sonnet aboard. Sonnet stepped into the boat and took a seat near the stern. Then her hand reached out, and grabbed the tiller.

"I remember this feeling. I miss this feeling."

"Sit tight." I started the small outboard engine, removed the sail covers and untied the lines.

"Sonnet, do you want to steer?"

"A blind woman steering? Sure, why not."

"I'll call out the maneuvers."

"Okay, let's try it. By the way, what's her name," asked Sonnet?

"*Sea Pup*, what else." A tear formed in her eye, and roll down her cheek.

"Great name."

"I know." I put the engine in gear and *Sea Pup*

moved forward.

"We need to go to starboard, Sonnet."

"Got it."

"Hold that. Now center her up." Sonnet moved the tiller perfectly. "Keep her straight and into the wind. I'll raise the sails." I looked back at Sonnet. She was so confident. She looked natural at the helm.

Once the sails were up I instructed her to bring *Sea Pup* to starboard 40°, which she did with incredible accuracy. *Sea Pup* heeled slightly. Sonnet smiled.

"Michael, I'm in heaven."

"No Sonnet, you're in Hampton." We laughed.

"How am I doing?"

"Perfectly." I looked at her hand. She had two fingers over the top of the tiller. She was feeling the water pressure on the rudder. She knew she was totally in touch with the boat and the sea. Then the wind shifted and the sails started to luff. Sonnet heard the sound of the luffing sails and moved the tiller appropriately. I gazed at her in amazement.

For the next two hours we sailed in Hampton Roads. Sonnet maintained the tiller throughout. "Michael, this is a great gift to be able to sail with my brother again. You've made me feel so young again." "Thanks. I was just thinking the same thing." We fell into another period of silence.

Sailing Again

"Michael, I had another dream last night."

"What about?"

"Audrey."

"Tell me about the dream."

"She was standing in front of a small house. The house looked like it had been badly damaged. There were some palm trees in the background."

"Sonnet, I have also seen that in my flashes. What do you think is going on?"

"I don't know."

"Do you think it is a vision of the present or the future?" I asked.

"Future," she replied with surety.

"My feelings exactly."

"Any sense where," she asked.

"The Caribbean, most likely." We fell into another period of silence. By now three hours had passed and it was time to head for home.

"Michael, when you are sailing do you keep an eye out for speeding powerboats?"

"Oh, yeah. I don't want to die the way my parents did." By four o'clock I had brought Sonnet back to the assisted living center.

"Thanks again, Michael. You have made me the happiest blind woman alive." We hugged. A weird feeling came over me. She wasn't letting go. Then I felt the tears on my shoulder.

"Sorry, Pup."

"No problem, Sonnet."

In the Blink of an Eye

Punctuality is very important to the Sterns, so like a good son I arrived five minutes early. The smell of pot roast permeated the air and it was a good smell considering I had been fending for myself. I walked into the kitchen. "Hi Mom."

"Michael, how is my Bujew son?"

"Great." I walked over and kissed her.

"So what have you been up to?"

"Not much, volunteering at the food bank. I've also been volunteering at an assisted living center in Hampton."

"Doing what?"

"I'm helping out a blind lady."

"Nice, very Bujew."

The discussion was interrupted by my father, who walked into the kitchen.

"Michael, you're early."

"Only a few minutes."

"Up for a glass of wine?"

"Sure." As I tried to restart the discussion with Su the doorbell rang. It was Mick Dermot.

"Michael, get the door."

"Okay." I walked to the foyer and opened the door. "Mick Dermot, come in."

"Thanks."

"Any news on the black kid?"

"No, I am still working on it. But we do need to talk about another issue."

"What's that?"

Sailing Again

"Not now."

"Why not?"

"Okay, let's go out back."

We walked to the kitchen and picked up two glasses of wine and walked outside.

"Okay, Mick Dermot, what's up?"

"I've continued to look into the accident that took Jost's life."

"Yeah. What did you find out?"

"There was another person in the car with Jost and Sonnet."

"Really, who?"

"Her name was Janet Jones."

"Interesting that Sonnet never mentioned that. So what about her?"

"According to Jackie Vee, she was Jost's girlfriend."

"So what else?"

"I think she had a child."

"Jost's child?"

"I don't know. I'm still researching."

"Very interesting."

"So what are you guys talking about," my father said as he approached us?

"Nothing, just catching up on some legal issues. Here's to your health." We raised our glasses.

"Cheers."

"Cheers."

Dinner proceed along as it had for hundreds

of times since Stephen and Anne Kenney's death, except now I wasn't asked to leave the table after dessert. Mick Dermot was finalizing some legal work that would transfer one third of my assets or $1 million to the Sterns. They were not yet aware of this.

"Well, I think I'll head home. Mom, great meal."

"Michael you're always running off."

"I have a busy day tomorrow."

"Before you go, grab your mail. It in a plastic bag in the kitchen."

"Will do."

Chapter 15

Audrey

The bag of mail opened as I tossed it on the bed. Junk mail made up 60 percent, bills 39 percent, and a letter with no return address made up the remaining 1 percent. The letter had a postmark that was not legible, but the stamp was from a foreign country. There was a picture of Queen Elizabeth on it and above her head there were three letters-- ECU--Eastern Caribbean Union. ECU members were those Caribbean islands either under UK control or who were formerly UK colonies.

"Audrey," I said out loud. I opened the letter and immediately looked at the bottom last two words. "Love, Audrey." Son of a gun. Sonnet was

In the Blink of an Eye

right. I placed the letter back into the envelope and placed it on my dresser.

When morning came, I woke up refreshed. I had no dreams, no sounds, no images. I walked to the dresser and picked up the letter and then put it down again. "I think I will read it over a cup of coffee," I said. I didn't rush to make the coffee. By 10 a.m. I was showered and dressed and the coffee was ready. Now it was time to face Audrey. I opened the letter and started to read.

Dear Michael,

It has taken a lot of courage for me to write you at this time. I know there are a lot of unanswered questions that have been rolling around in your mind but don't expect all the answers. Maybe I can answer them the next time we see each other, if there is a next time. But like you, who has questions, I have questions too. We need to deal with my questions first if there is any chance of reconnecting.

I really miss you and I believe you are missing me as well. But let me fill in a few blanks. Houghton Plantation is now in the hands of my brother. That happened as a result of my father's death and his will. Frankly, I'm glad I don't have to deal with that. I haven't spoken to him in several months so I don't know what has happened to the place or if it's been sold.

Audrey

I want to understand everything you know about Angel, the girl from the shack. After the day you freaked out at the shack, I went in and sat there and tried to see what you had seen. At first I saw nothing. Then one night as I was leaving, I felt a presence behind me. I turned around and there was a girl. She called out to me. She said, "Michael, Michael." And then I heard her say, "I'm not the demon child." Michael, she stared into my eyes and I stared back. She scared the hell out of me. Why are her eyes like yours? Who is Angel and why does she call out your name? Somehow I have become part of your insanity. I know you see things and hear things. I think I was getting too close so you pushed me away. Your secret was safe with me. Teach me how you do this and why you do this. Michael, I have felt very empty since we broke up and I know I want to see you, I just don't know if I should. Please write back. I miss you.

Love,
Audrey

I put the letter down. I felt sick and conflicted. I now knew that she had gotten too close and I was right to push her away. I also worried that it might have been a decision that I would always regret.

The next day I returned to the assisted living center to see Sonnet. She was in the garden when

In the Blink of an Eye

I arrived.

"Good morning, Sis."

"Morning, Pup. So did you hear from Audrey?"

"Yes, I got a letter last night."

"Is everything all right?"

"No, not exactly. She clearly knows about my ability to see back in time. She has also seen Angel Lehcar."

"How?"

"As a ghost image in the shack. She hinted that Angel has eyes like Pup's."

"You mean like yours."

"She wants to know everything."

"What are you going to do?"

"I don't know. She didn't confirm that she was living in the Caribbean but that's where the stamp was purchased."

"Interesting"

"Sonnet, I have a question to ask you."

"What?"

"Tell me about Janet Jones. I understand she was in the accident and Jackie Vee says she was Jost's girlfriend. And also tell me why you never mentioned her to me."

"Janet was trouble."

"In what way?"

"She had Jost under her spell and was not faithful. She was a love him and leave him kind of girl."

"Is it true that she had a child?"

"Yes, there was a child."

"Was it Jost's child?"

"No," she said with great agitation.

"How do you know?"

"She said so. And besides, Jost never said the child was his. Believe me, Michael, if that was my niece I would have never let her go."

"How would you have raised a child?"

"I would have found a way. Please don't pursue this any further. It will only make you crazy."

"You're probably right."

"So, Michael, when will you take me sailing again?"

Later that night I sat looking at the snow on my used TV set and wondered whether Sonnet was really telling the truth.

In the Blink of an Eye

Chapter 16

Angel: Bossman

Bossman had two things he'd become proficient in. One was keeping the workers (slaves) in line and the other was rape. Bossman was a free black man who grew intolerable of everything. No one was really sure how he became free but it was said that his owner died of natural causes. Normally a slave would have been given to an owner's family members, but all the other family members had moved up north and had no need for slave labor.

Bossman kept the whip on his hip and wasn't afraid to use it. Sometimes he would make me watch the whippings. Sometimes he would make me treat the wounds, especially when it was my

In the Blink of an Eye

brother who was getting the whippings. The women rarely got whipped. We got our punishment the other way. It didn't matter if you were married or not. If you did anything that displeased Bossman, he would have his way with you. Sometimes he would rape the women in the barn, sometimes in the fields. Some of the women would kill themselves rather than face another rape or beating. Some never married because the men feared the punishment that would follow if a man looked lovingly on a woman. Most women had many children. Most of them came from Bossman.

My mother and father had wed before Bossman came to the plantation. My brother was born two years before me. He was tall, like my father, and had broad shoulders and muscular arms. He was handsome and attracted the looks of many young women. Bossman hated him. I think it was a jealous feeling. However, as my brother got to his teenage years his look changed from the scars that populated his back, legs, neck and face. These were whipping scars.

Any man that challenged Bossman was gone. How they were killed or where they were killed was a mystery. One night Father woke to the sounds of yelling. The yelling was not uncommon but that night was different because my mother was gone. He walked out of the shack and walked toward the house. The yelling grew louder. Then he walked

Angel: Bossman

to the barn and peered into the window. Mother was being beaten. She was nude. Bossman was about to reach for his whip when Father kicked in the barn door and confronted Bossman. The battle only lasted a few seconds before Bossman pulled a large knife from his belt and slashed Father's neck, hitting the jugular vein. Father fell to his feet. Bossman kicked him in the face and then proceeded to rape my mother. My brother and I watched the whole thing. From that day on I pledged to avenge Father's death.

After Father was gone, the whippings became more frequent and by the time my brother was 16 he was, for all purposes, mentally dead. He would walk around in a trance, never speaking, never smiling and barely working. Soon after, he disappeared. Mother said very little. She lived in total fear that I would be Bossman's next victim, but I came to realize that I was special in his eyes.

Now that George Lehcar and Little George were out of the way it became easier for Bossman to exploit us. On so many nights Bossman would walk into the shack and summon Mother.

"Let's go, Rose, it's time," Bossman would say. Mother would say nothing. She obeyed his commands. She was doing what it took to keep Bossman away from me. And when Mother would return, Bossman would say, "How's that demon child of yours doing?"

In the Blink of an Eye

"Her name is Angel," Mother would repeatedly tell him.

"She looks like a demon to me. Only the devil makes a child with eyes like that."

Every time Mother was escorted to the barn, I would lie awake, fantasizing that I was killing Bossman. Sometimes I would dream that all the women on the plantation would be fighting to see who would kill Bossman. And in those dreams I would yell out, "He is my kill, my kill, my kill!" By the time I was 20, Mother had started to act like Little George. She walked around in a trance, speechless and lifeless. She stopped eating and drinking and before long, she was gone. Some of the other women said she hung herself and others said she was hung by Bossman. Nevertheless she was gone.

Over the next several months, Bossman said very little to me. I minded my business, working very hard in the fields, picking cotton for the master. He was gone most of the time and I think if he knew how Bossman was treating his property, he may have confronted him. But he didn't.

Then one night my life changed.

"Demon girl, I want to see you up at the house after supper."

"Master's house?"

"Are you deaf?"

"No, Bossman."

"Clean up nice for me or get a whipping."

Angel: Bossman

"Yes, Bossman."

As I walked to the shack, I started to think about the best way to kill him. I assumed he was going to rape me. I thought about putting a knife in the haystack and when he wasn't watching, cutting his neck like he did to Father. I thought about slicing him up with an ax blade or shooting him with a rifle. Somehow he would be my kill.

I put on my best dress. It was the one Mother made for me to wear to church. Then I walked to Master's house. I'd never been in the house before. Slaves were not allowed in the master's house. I knocked on the door and walked in. The house was smaller inside than I expected. The furnishings were beautiful compared to the shack or compared to where Bossman lived. There was a coolness that was immediately apparent. There were paintings on the walls and rugs on the floor. The cotton business must've been good.

Bossman walked into the foyer. "Demon child, you are prettier than your mother." I said nothing.

"Didn't your mother teach you any manners?"

"Yes, Bossman, thank you."

"Demon child, sit down." He pointed to a chair in the parlor.

"Are we allowed in the Master's house?"

"Not your problem." I said nothing.

"I've been reluctant to have my way with you. I don't like the way you stare at me with those eyes.

In the Blink of an Eye

I think you're a child of the Devil. Maybe so. Don't matter, I'm going to Hell anyway."

Chapter 17

Angel:
Temporary Peace

Over the next few months there was peace on the plantation. The master was back and that meant Bossman had to control his temper and his desires. Unfortunately, Master's presence didn't last long enough. With Master gone again, Bossman quickly went back to his ways.

My plan to kill Bossman expanded with each day. During the harvest I would collect sharp sticks which I would harden over the cooking fire. On occasions I would find pieces of glass or metal and hide them in places where I expected the rapes to occur. I had become so obsessed with the kill that there were 30 or so weapons planted in and around

In the Blink of an Eye

the barn. I was never so prepared for anything in my life.

As early winter arrived, the harvest slowed and so did Bossman. He seemed less angry and continued to keep his distance from me, which only helped me continue my mission to hide weapons. I waited for my chance to eventually avenge Father's murder. Winter was now in full force and life on the plantation moved from planting and harvesting to sewing and canning. Bossman had stayed away for the most part which meant both he and I were safe. Then on a cold Sunday morning, he appeared at the entrance to the shack.

"Demon girl, pretty up and come to the house."

"Yes, Bossman." I ignored his request and showed up at the house as I was. I walked in and waited in the foyer. Bossman appeared.

"Into the room," he said, pointing to the parlor. "Sit down." Once again I said nothing. "Demon girl--" I cut him off in mid-sentence.

"My name is Angel."

"Fine, Angel. The good news is I'm not going to beat you. The bad news is . . ." I tried not to hear it. "Pull up your dress." I sat frozen. "Don't make me hurt you." I remained frozen. Then out of nowhere, his fist flew into my chest, removing any bit of air. I gasped. "Off with the dress." The dress came off. He threw me onto the ground and raped me. I felt nothing other than the mounting hate and belief that the future would taste so wonderful once I succeeded in my kill.

By the time I woke up from the numbness, Bossman was gone. I had no idea how much time had passed; all I knew was that the time for me to complete my deed was soon approaching. I got up and looked out the window. Bossman was walking to the barn with another young girl. He was dragging her behind him. This was my chance. I searched through the drawers in the kitchen and found two small knives, both which could be easily hidden under my clothing. I placed them in my undergarment and walked quietly to the shack. On the way, I could hear the screams from the barn and knew that yet another woman was being violated.

The weeks came and went and Bossman said nothing to me. Then sickness followed. One of the elder women examined me and told me she thought I was in a motherly state. This was devastating; the thought of carrying Bossman's child, knowing that I would kill my child's father. By month four of the pregnancy, I started to show. Bossman took notice.

"Demon girl, is that my baby in there?"

"Yes, Bossman."

"Take good care of the baby."

"I will, Bossman."

In the Blink of an Eye

"If that baby has devil eyes, I'll kill it. It better have brown eyes like me."

"I hope so, Bossman." More months drifted by and with each month, I grew bigger and bigger.

The planting season seemed to go by like the passing of a single day. The harvest was soon upon us and the elder women started to teach me how to prepare for birth. On one beautiful morning in September I started labor and by afternoon, the baby was born. As the baby came into the world, I wondered about its future but the ultimate question was about the eyes. The baby was placed on my stomach and I stared at him. His eyes were dark brown. The baby was safe. The next day Bossman came to the shack.

"How's that baby of mine?"

"Fine, Bossman."

"I heard his eyes are brown."

"Yes, Bossman."

"I want that baby to have my name."

"Whatever you say, Bossman." Then he left. So with the baby now born and named, it was time to accelerate my plan.

Chapter 18

Angel:
The Act

The planting season was upon us again and I worked the fields with the other women. Our babies, most of them Bossman's, were strapped on our backs as we worked in the springtime air.

"Liza." She looked up at me. "I'm going to kill Bossman."

"Hush your words, child. That's a sin. You'll go to Hell for killing him."

"I think we are in Hell now."

"How are you fixin' to kill him?"

"Like he killed my father."

"There are many girls who would like to do that."

In the Blink of an Eye

"Do you want to help me?"

"No, girl, I'm no sinner."

"Emma." She looked up at me. "I'm going to kill Bossman."

"How?"

"I got my ways."

"You need help?"

"Yes."

"Count me in."

"Do you think we'll go to Hell for this?"

"No, Angel. You may land in Heaven for killing the evil bastard."

"Josie, I'm going to kill Bossman."

"How?"

"I got that covered."

"That's a sin, Angel."

"Don't you think God wants me to kill him?"

"No, but count me in."

Throughout the day the word spread in the fields and before the day was out all four women I told about my plan agreed to help me fulfill my mission. The plan was simple; four women with rocks and one with a knife. Each woman would prepare a sockwhip. This involves placing small rocks in a long sock which when swung at the face would inflict severe damage. With four women swinging sockwhips at Bossman's face, one would expect for him to be injured enough for me to make the final kill, my kill. We decided to hit at dusk as the light

Angel: The Act

of day was disappearing. Bossman would expect all of us to be in our shacks. He'd be on the prowl for a rape victim. We didn't know who. What was for certain, the next attempted rape would be his last.

It was the night of the next full moon. Then it happened. Bossman came after Liza. He was half drunk and the look of violence never looked so strong. Liza was calm. She knew he would never complete his act. She walked into the barn with Bossman. Then the shack doors opened one by one and the women emerged with four sockwhips and two knives. The barn door was opened slightly as I looked in. Liza was lying on a blanket that was draped over several bales of hay. Bossman stared at her. He staggered a bit from the alcohol he had taken. Then he loosened his belt and dropped his pants. He staggered again. Bossman was regaining his balance when he heard the barn door open. He spun around and reached for his whip but lost his balance and fell to the ground. Liza jumped up and kicked dirt in his face. Emma delivered the first blow. The sockwhip flew into Bossman's face. The impact shattered his nose. The second blast hit his eyes, splitting his eyebrow. The third hit his teeth, shattering most of them. The final blow was across the back of his neck which sent him into unconsciousness. In 20 seconds the giant was disarmed. He lay there helpless, totally open and exposed for the final act.

In the Blink of an Eye

"Liza, get the rope and tie his hands and ankles. Then tie another rope around his chest."

"Why not do it here?"

"We need to hide the body away from the plantation." The rope that was tied around his chest was then tied to a 20-foot lead which was secured to one of the horses.

"Let's go." Over the next half-hour, we dragged Bossman through the fields until he got to the edge of the plantation.

"What are all these mounds?" asked Liza.

"Burial sites, I guess. I wonder which one of these is the resting place of my family."

"Emma, get the water." Emma opened up a jar of water that she carried from the barn.

"Wake him up." Emma poured the water on Bossman's face until he woke. His eyes opened slowly.

"What happened? Where am I? Who are you?"

"Bossman, it's time for you to pay for your sins; the rapes and murders."

"Demon girl?"

"My name is Angel." He closed his eyes.

"Bossman, how do you want to die?" He said nothing. "I said, how do you want to die?"

"Demon girl, you'll go to Hell for this."

"Wrong, Bossman. God's on my side on this one. So do you want it slow and painful or quick

Angel: The Act

and painless?"

"Quick and painless."

"Wrong answer, Bossman." And with that, the sockwhip was swung into Bossman's crotch.

"That's for raping my mother." Then the act was repeated.

"That's for whipping my brother." Bossman screamed out in pain.

"And the next will be for killing my father." And with that said, I pulled out the two kitchen knives and held them up to the moonlight and started to chant.

"My kill, my kill, my kill." The chanting grew louder. "My kill, my kill, my kill." The chanting continued until it became hypnotic. And in the end and in a moment of total euphoria, I descended on Bossman running a knife into each side of his neck. The blood shot out like a geyser, covering my hands and arms. I pressed the blades further into his neck until the blade tips met. Bossman's heart stopped within seconds. Silence fell over us. I could feel my heart pounding and could feel all my fear evaporate. The act was done.

In the Blink of an Eye

Chapter 19

Angel:
The Consequence

The next three days came and went; no Boss-man, no Master Paulson. The workers continued to work out in the fields unsupervised. None of the slaves ran away. We didn't know where to go anyway, having never been off the plantation. On the fourth day, Master Paulson arrived back at the plantation and found no Bossman. He rode his horse out to the fields asking us if we knew what happened to him.

"Master Paulson, I think Bossman ran off," I said in my most convincing voice.

"No chance of that, I owed him too much wages. If there was a mutiny among you, someone will

In the Blink of an Eye

pay." He turned away and rode to the edge of the plantation.

"I wonder why he is riding out there?" one of the girls asked.

"That's where all the killing has been done."

That night Master Paulson assembled most of the adults.

"I'm prepared to whip each of you, one by one, if you don't tell me who killed Radcliffe." Silence fell over us. Then he pulled out a gun and pointed it at Emma.

"I'll ask you one more time. Who killed Radcliffe?" No one said a word. He cocked back the hammer of his revolver. Emma closed her eyes.

"Do you want me to pull the trigger?"

"Master Paulson, I did it. I killed Bossman." He uncocked his gun. Emma opened her eyes and looked at me.

"It was my kill, Master Paulson," I said in a tone of no regret.

"Why did you do this?"

"He killed my family, he raped the women, and he deserved to die."

"Maybe so, but that is my decision, not yours.

Everyone back to your shacks. Miss Lehcar, you stay here."

The slaves moved quickly. I grabbed Emma's arm as she passed by me. "Take care of my baby."

Angel: The Consequence

"I will, don't worry."

Soon after the crowd dispersed, Master led me to the barn and shackled me to a barn post. "I'll deal with you in the morning."

The next two days, I stayed shackled in the barn while Master supervised the workers. The following day I was awakened by Rush.

"Wake up, Angel."

"Rush, what are you doing here?"

"Master made me the foreman. It will be a new day on the plantation. The killing and the raping is over."

"What about me?"

"I'm sorry, Angel." And with that, he turned his back and walked away.

"Rush, tell me." He stopped and turned around.

"Master is going to turn you over to the local judge in Elizabeth City County. You're going to be tried for murder. Angel," he paused. "I think you need to prepare to meet your family in Heaven." He started to walk away, then stopped and turned to me. "You've done a great thing for us. Thank you and may God look out for you."

The trip to the courthouse took two days. Master took me by wagon rather than have me walk. Walking would have taken too long.

"Angel Lehcar, is that your name?" the judge asked.

In the Blink of an Eye

"Yes sir."

"Mr. Paulson says you admitted killing Radcliffe Brown. Is that true?"

"Yes sir."

"I also understand that Radcliffe Brown was your husband. Is that correct?"

"No sir. He was the father of my baby but he raped me."

"Miss Lehcar, there are no laws that protect slaves from that but there are laws that protect free men, black or white."

"He killed my parents and my brother."

"No laws protecting slaves. The owner has to deal with those matters. Miss Lehcar, what is your child's name?"

"Radcliffe Brown Jr."

"And who will take care of him, now that his father was murdered and you are likely to hang?"

"Miss Emma, back on the plantation."

"Very well." The judge continued, "Miss Lehcar, if convicted you will be put to death. Do you have any preference as to the method?"

"No sir."

"Mr. Paulson, do you have a preference?"

"No, Your Honor."

"Miss Lehcar, as you admitted to the murder of Radcliffe Brown, I hereby sentence you to death by hanging. It will occur tomorrow at noon. Tomorrow you will have the opportunity to say your last

Angel: The Consequence

words. Think hard about what you want to say as you leave this world." The hammer fell and court was adjourned. It was that quick and simple. You kill a free man, you're put to death. There was no jury for slaves. In the eyes of the court, we had the same rights as a street dog.

I never fell asleep that night. I just stared at the cell door wishing I was free but I had no regrets, other than orphaning my child. At 11:30 I was escorted to the hanging platform, which was constructed behind the courthouse. As I stood there, the trap door in the floor was opened and closed and tested and retested to ensure a proper hanging. The noose was placed over my head and neck.

"Angel Lehcar, do you have any last words?" the executioner stated.

"Yes sir."

"Proceed."

"May I have my hands untied just for a moment?"

"Very well." I slowly dropped to my knees and raised my hands out to the heavens and started to chant the words of my avengement.

"My kill, my kill, my kill, my kill."

The executioner retied my hands. I kept chanting, "My kill, my kill." The noose was placed over my head and around my neck. "My kill, my kill, my kill." The noose was tightened to the point that I could feel the rope pressing on my throat. "My

In the Blink of an Eye

kill, my kill, my kill, my kill, my kill, my kill." And the door was released.

That afternoon, a notice was placed on the courtroom board.

Today, Angel Lehcar was put to death for the murder of Radcliffe Brown. She will be buried in the public cemetery on East Mellen Street in the Village of Phoebus.

Chapter 20

Back on East
Mellen Street

I had been very busy working on East Mellen
Street, volunteering for a local arts organization.
The director of the organization, Paul Curry, and I
had become good friends. A foundation had been
formed to raise money for a renovation project that
would convert an old movie theater into a perform-
ing arts center. I helped launch the project with a
sizable gift. It was money well spent.

"Paul, what do you know about the old cemetery at the end of East Mellen Street?"

"I think it was an old public cemetery. I believe that's where the slaves were buried who were
convicted of crimes. One of the local colleges did

a study of old burial sites. There are a lot of slave sites around here."

"When did it become part of the church property?"

"I don't know. Why are you so interested in that old cemetery?"

"It's a very long story. By the way, I'm going to D.C. next week and see the monks. Do you want to come along?"

Paul paused, looking for a reply. "Count me in."

"Great."

As the day came to a close, Paul and I headed off in our own directions. I decided to take a look at the cemetery on East Mellen Street. The cemetery was small and many of the stones looked like they had once fallen down and were reset in the soil. Many dated back to pre-Civil War days. There were a few of them that looked more current, but it was clear that no one had been buried there in the last 20 years. I walked slowly to the end of the graves looking for Angel's stone but none of the stones bore her name. At the end of the last row is where I found Jost's stone. Sonnet said he was buried here but never explained why this spot was chosen. The stone was very old looking as if it was engraved more than a hundred years earlier. It simply read "Jost Alexson 1920 - December 10, 1960." I continued to search for Angel but found noth-

Back on East Mellen Street

ing. As I walked away in disappointment, I looked back at the cemetery, making a final glance at Jost's stone. Then I stopped and squinted at the back of the stone. Was there something there? I returned to Jost's grave site, staring at the back side of the stone. Were there letters on the back, I thought to myself.

I took out my handkerchief and started to rub the stone clean. I thought I could see the letter "A" but the stone was covered with too much moss. I walked down the street to the East Mellen Hardware Store and purchased a small wire brush. Then I returned to the cemetery. Very carefully I removed the algae, moss, mud, and dirt that had accumulated over the years. I wet my fingers and started to rub the stone. Letter by letter started to appear but were unrecognizable until I stood over the stone and looked down from above. There it was, Angel Lehcar. Each letter lay upside-down when viewed head-on. If this was her stone, then she must have been buried opposite Jost. They shared the same stone.

"Unbelievable," I said aloud. "Two graves, one stone. Reincarnate buried together." I looked down the row of stones. There were no other stones engraved on the back side. Angel must have been the lone person buried in the row.

I drove to the assisted living center. When I

arrived, Sonnet was not in her room. A nurse approached me.

"Mr. Kenney?"

"Where's Sonnet?"

"I have some bad news," the nurse said.

"What? Where's Sonnet?" I was now getting agitated.

"Miss Sonnet had a stroke. They took her to the hospital downtown." I ran out of the facility and drove to the hospital. A hospital volunteer sat at the front desk.

"Can you tell me what room Sonnet Alexson is in?" The volunteer looked through the list.

"She is in the ICU. Are you family?"

"Yes, I am her brother."

"We have limited visiting hours in the ICU."

"Sure, whatever."

I ran to the elevator. "Come on, come on," I said impatiently. The door opened. I pressed the button for the fourth floor and waited for the doors to close. The elevator lurched and started its slow climb three floors. A few seconds later the door opened. The ICU was down the hall. I pressed the entry intercom.

"Yes, how can I help you?"

"I would like to see Sonnet Alexson." The buzzer rang and the door to the ICU opened. I walked to the desk.

"Are you here to see Miss Alexson?"

Back on East Mellen Street

"Yes." I followed the nurse past several rooms until I got to the one Sonnet was in. Standing next to her bed was a short, thin man. He had a bible in his hand and was praying. He looked at me.

"Are you family of the deceased?"

"What did you say?"

"Are you family of Miss Alexson?"

"Yes, I am her brother." He looked at me strangely noticing the 40-year difference in age.

"Miss Alexson passed away a few moments ago. I'm sorry."

"May I have some time with her alone?"

"Yes. Of course." I slid the glass door closed behind him. I moved a chair next to the bed and sat down. I put my hand on her arm.

"Sonnet, it's Pup."

"Pup, I'm sorry," I heard a voice say. I looked over my shoulder.

"Michael, thank you for the joy you have brought me. I must go see Jost." I scanned the room. There was no one there. Then I felt a familiar sensation. I turned my head to the left and looked at my shoulder. In front of my eyes, a wet spot started to appear.

"Sonnet's tears," I said softly. Then I felt a hand on my other shoulder. I stood up and turned to see Sonnet standing there. She was translucent and shimmering. She smiled and started to speak to me but I could not hear what she was saying. Then her

In the Blink of an Eye

image started to fade until she had totally vanished. I collapsed onto the chair. Then I reached out my hand and touched her arm again. It was ice cold. For the next two hours I sat with Sonnet, trying to understand why she was taken from me.

The next day I returned to the assisted living facility to speak to Sonnet's nurse.

"Mr. Kenney, we are all so sad about Ms. Sonnet passing."

"Thanks."

"You know you really made her happy over the last several months. You gave her hope about seeing her brother again. And she hadn't stopped talking about the sailing trip you and she did last month. You made her a very happy woman."

"Do you know how she wants to be taken care of?"

"Cremation, I think. I know she recently met with an attorney about her will."

"Really. Do you know who?"

"I don't know his name but he was about 60 years old and walked with a slight hitch."

"Mick Dermott," I thought to myself.

It took me less than 10 minutes to get to Mick Dermott's office. I was angry that he never said anything about an issue he knew would be so important to me. I walked into his lobby like I owned the place, passed right by his assistant, and walked into his office. He was on the phone.

"Let me call you back," he said abruptly. "Michael, you look angry. Sit down. I have the information on Richard Brown, the guy that was killed in the accident with Jost. Remember, I told you his mother may have worked for the Kenneys." I cut him off in mid-sentence.

"When were you going to tell me that Sonnet was your client?"

"Attorney-client privilege."

"Don't give me that crap."

"Calm down, Michael."

"Don't tell me to calm down, Mickey. I want answers and I want them now."

"Okay, what do you want to know?"

"Why did Sonnet hire you?"

"She wanted to change her will."

"Why?"

"She wanted to add you as an alternate beneficiary."

"What the hell is that?"

"If she left her estate to someone who predeceases you, then you get the assets in the estate."

"Okay, fine. Who was the primary beneficiary?"

"Michael, you are going too far."

"Dammit, Mick Dermott, let me guess; the daughter of Janet Jones, Sonnet's niece and my daughter." Our eyes locked on each other. There was an extended pause and then Mick Dermott sighed.

"Yes, Janet Jones' daughter. Her name is Emily Jones."

"You know her name," I said, nearly shouting. "How did you get that information?"

"It was provided to me by Sonnet."

"I knew she lied to me. Do you know where she is?"

"No, Sonnet never saw her after the accident. She basically disappeared."

"Find her. I don't care how much it costs. Find her."

"Believe me, I will. I promise. So do you want to hear about Richard Brown?"

"Sure."

"Richard Brown is not his real name. His birth certificate reads Radcliffe Brown IV."

"Radcliffe Brown?"

"Yes."

"That's amazing."

Mick Dermott was never able to locate Emily Jones. Despite the efforts of Mick, the FBI, and the IRS, Emily Jones was never found. As for the will, Sonnet Alexson was cremated. Her ashes were divided in half. One half was spread in the Chesapeake Bay and the other half was spread over Pup's grave. All of her belongings including ap-

Back on East Mellen Street

proximately $100,000 were given to charity, with the exception of her pictures and the necklace that once belonged to her grandmother. Those items were placed in a safety deposit box for safekeeping.

In the Blink of an Eye

Part Two
The Future

"While the past is the most tangible element of
time; It is the future that ranks second as we
tend to shape the future around our knowledge
of the past."

"It is the present that we are unable to touch."

In the Blink of an Eye

Chapter 21

Blink Flash

Something happened to me after Sonnet's death. Something happened that was so profound, it changed my life in ways no one could ever explain or imagine. Only I knew why it happened. The months following Sonnet's death were very difficult. I spent most of my time either in D.C. at the temple or on East Mellen Street working with Paul Curry. Paul had become a frequent visitor to the temple and found a spiritual home there. I continued to meditate, trying to understand the next phase of my life and how it would play out.

For approximately two years I could not invoke an image flash. At night I dreamt in silence. I was

In the Blink of an Eye

in a vacuum. I tried to blame it on the mediation but that was a cheap excuse. The fact was that my discovery of my past was fulfilled and my discovery of the future was in limbo. And there was the unanswered question about the image flash I had of Audrey as she stood in front of the destroyed island home. That was my only glimpse of the future.

Two years had passed and much had changed on East Mellen Street. The theater was now open and doing well. The shop where I bought the snow TV was gone and the church cemetery where Angel, Jost and Sonnet lay was under major renovation. There was a real sense of new life that was being felt on the street. I decided to take a break and went to D.C. to spend time with the monks. This time Su came with me. I felt a need to reconnect with the woman who introduced me to the monks and to the Bujew. For four days we meditated. Each meditation session lasted three to five hours. Jodii joined us in meditation. On the last day, Jodii took me aside.

"Michael, you are like a stranger to me. What is happening to you?"

"Jodii, I'm locked in the present."

"The present doesn't exist but only for a brief moment, Michael."

"I know. Once I saw an image of the future. I need to see more. My old methods are not working. I see nothing and I hear nothing."

Blink Flash

"So, this means you have not gotten over Sonnet's death. Go home and continue to meditate. You are near the end of your journey and will soon start another. I can feel it."

"I'll take your advice, old friend." Then I handed him an envelope for the temple. It was money well spent.

The next week came and went with no change. Then on a hot, humid night in August the future began to reveal itself. The weather forecaster called for severe thunderstorms. I decided I wanted to see the storms unobstructed and drove to Grandview.

Once there, I reached into my pocket and pulled out a packet of sand that was given to me by Jodii. I held it in my hands and stared out into the darkness of the Chesapeake Bay. Then the first bolt of lightning exploded from the clouds. Then another and another until the sky came alive with a constant flicker. I continued to stare out on the Bay. I looked into the rearview mirror of my car and could see flashes of lightning bolts appear on my eyeballs. Then a huge streak of lightning crossed the sky. Then I saw her in the flash. Audrey. Then another flash from the sky; a black man with dreadlocks. Another lightning bolt appeared; a young girl with blonde hair. Then a man and a telescope and then Audrey again. The flashes of light continued as the image jumped across my eyes. Then a flash and the sound of wind. Then

In the Blink of an Eye

another flash and the sound of a fierce gust. Then the sky went dark and the lightning stopped and so did the flashes. Jodii was right: the future was just around the corner.

I started my drive back to Queen Street and decided to call Su on the cell phone.

"Hello."

"Hi, Mom. Did you see the storm? The lightning was fantastic."

"Storm? There was no storm. Your father and I were just out for a walk. The sky was as clear as it could be. The stars were everywhere."

"Mom, you didn't see the lightning and hear the wind?"

"No, Michael. Where were you?"

"I was in Grandview."

"That's only around the corner from us."

"I know. Are you sure you didn't see the lightning?"

"We didn't see a single flash. Michael, get some rest. You seem very stressed."

"No Mom, just the opposite. I feel free."

Chapter 22

Back in the Game

Night after night I lay on my bed staring at the fan. Image flash after image flash occurred. I was back in the game, seeing images, hearing dream sounds and writing in my journal. The addiction was back and I was happy to be reacquainted with an old friend. Part of the joy came from what I was seeing: Audrey. I could tell by the images that she had aged only a few years. She was still as beautiful as I remembered her. But there were many new faces and sounds and I couldn't help but wonder if one of them might have been Emily Jones. But within the joy there were a few things that started to bother me. One was the guilt for never having

In the Blink of an Eye

responded to Audrey's letter, a letter that was nearly three years old. The second was that I was starting to have occasional struggles with forgetfulness, something I do recall was at issue for Pup.

The 1980s were long gone and the 1990s were upon me. I continued to live on Queen Street next to the sail loft and I continued to volunteer in the community and share my wealth with others. I grew closer to Allen and Su as friends rather than parents, spending time sailing on the Bay. I also started to take a real interest in the weather as so many of my images and dream sounds suggested that weather would play a major role in the future. While asleep, I could hear the names of boys and girls and wondered if they might be the names of a hurricane or typhoon. Only time would tell.

It was now 1995 and I had been documenting the future for three years. I had a pretty good idea what was in store for me; I just didn't know when the future would become the present. Six out of seven days a week I would sort through the mail, always wondering if Audrey would write me again. I also checked weekly at Su and Allen's house to see if any mail came in from the Caribbean. So once again, I sorted through the mail; electric bill, gas bill, Visa bill, junk mail, junk mail, Audrey. I looked at the letter. My hand was shaking. The postmark was six months old. The letter

Back in the Game

was originally addressed to Su and Allen's house but the Postal Service stamp indicated that it was to be forwarded to me. Instead it was delivered to a wrong address in Hampton and once rejected there, was returned to the Caribbean. It was then resent to the U.S. and once again was forwarded to the wrong address. This cycle occurred two more times. Finally it appeared in my mailbox, obviously hand-delivered by the Hampton resident who had gotten the letter four times. On the envelope was a message from him to me: "I'm sick of getting this letter, I hope it's yours."

I sat on the couch and opened the letter and removed the contents. It was not a letter at all. There was no greeting or salutation. Inscribed on the paper was a poem from Audrey.

Sometimes I glimpse your heart abandoned near the harbor
Though your life is tidy now and under control
Still I see the shadow of the soul you left behind
As your life goes on in the freedom that you stole.

Time rushes by now with sunrises and sunsets
We call back days just to keep alive our youth
If our passions wear a mantle of silver streaks
Can we finally be let in on the truth?

How does a phantom measure time and tide?
What you left unsaid, and I left undone
So now if you were stranded, on a desert island,
And could choose a friend, I wouldn't be that one.

In the Blink of an Eye

Still if I could bewitch you with a howling wind call,
Bring you back here beneath the fabled mountain's lee
And make your stay here safe and healing,
Through lifting ocean mists would you finally see?

That those days were like a branding
They burnt the heart and seared the soul
So your absence leaves a raw wound
And since you left our shores, we can't be whole.

So come back to the battered harbor
You'll find the old lighthouse doesn't burn alone
There are many beacons still kept blazing
Just to guide your way back home.

Soon you'll find that heart you abandoned by the harbor
Your crazy life could explode and stagger out of control
As the crashing water wind of the islands
Grabs your destiny's dice and lets it roll.

Line by line I read the poem, looking for some hidden meanings. But the meaning wasn't hidden at all. It was right in front of me, plain for me to see. It was beautifully written and to the point. There was no doubt that I hurt her deeply and in a very personal way. And I realized at that moment that she had moved on. I lay down and stared at the ceiling fan. In some ways I was glad we were done with each other and that she had gone off in her own direction. But inside I knew I let a very special person slip through my fingers; a person who I still loved. Why didn't I make her a priority? Did I think she would wait forever for me to

Back in the Game

solidify my feeling? I put the poem back in the envelope and placed it next to the other letter that was stored in my sock drawer.

In the Blink of an Eye

Chapter 23

Weather or Not

The Cape Verde Islands lie off the western coast of Africa. I have heard that the Cape Verdian women are extraordinarily beautiful, a genetic combination of Portuguese and Sub-Sahara African. The islands are both rich and poor. They are poor in the economic sense and rich in weather sense. Cape Verde and the coast of Africa is the birthplace of hurricanes that move from the east toward the west, often descending on the Caribbean islands and the southern U.S.

I had recently gotten cable TV and became accustomed to watching the Weather Channel as I ate my breakfast.

In the Blink of an Eye

"There are a few tropical systems forming just west of the Cape Verde Islands. We'll watch them and give you updated weather information on the progress of these storms," the weather forecasters said.

"Interesting," I thought. The next day I repeated my routine—bowl of cereal and milk and the Weather Channel.

"The tropical depressions we talked about yesterday are gaining strength. If they mature into tropical storms, they will be named Tropical Storm Dennis and Tropical Storm Ellen."

"That's it, I'm out of here."

I ran into my bedroom, took out a duffel bag from underneath my bed and started to pack. A half-hour later I was on the phone with the travel agent.

"I'm looking to purchase a one-way ticket to Sint Maarten."

"Okay. Do you have any specific dates?" the travel agent asked.

"I'll take the next flight out of either Norfolk or Richmond." She put me on hold. I glanced at Audrey's last letter, the postmark read Sint Maarten. Then the agent returned to the phone.

"There is a flight out this afternoon to New York. You will have to stay overnight and catch the morning flight to Sint Maarten."

"Fine, book it."

Weather or Not

"Don't you want to know the price?"

"No, just book it." I gave her all the particulars and just like that, I was bound for the future.

By 6 p.m. I was at the hotel just outside JFK Airport.

"Hello."

"Hi, Mom."

"Michael, how are you?"

"I'm going to Sint Maarten for a few weeks."

"Why?"

"I'm going to help out with the relief effort."

"What relief effort?"

"The hurricane in the Atlantic is heading that way."

"How do you know it will hit Sint Maarten?"

"I heard it in a dream." There was a long pause in the dialog.

"Call me when you get there and be careful."

"I will, Mom. Send my love to Dad." Then I hung up and called Paul and Jodii. The conversation seemed weirdly similar to the conversation I just had with Su.

When the alarm rang, I jumped out of bed and realized I wasn't home. The problem was that I couldn't remember where I was or why I was in a strange hotel room. I searched through my bag and pulled out the tickets. "Sint Maarten?" I fixed my eyes on the date and time and then looked at my watch. The plane was leaving in three hours.

In the Blink of an Eye

"I guess I know where I'm going." As I was shaving, I turned on the Weather Channel.

"When we come back we'll update you on hurricanes Dennis and Ellen," the weather forecaster announced. Then I remembered why I was going to Sint Maarten. I also remembered that my short-term memory was starting to fail periodically, a problem more common in older folks than someone in their early 30s.

"Damn, I need to see a doctor when I return to Hampton. Something's going bad up there," I said, thinking of my brain.

The flight to Sint Maarten was easy. I sat by myself in a three-seat row, writing in my journal and occasionally dosing off, only to be bombarded with the sound of storms, heavy rain, and fierce winds. Every once in a while I would hear voices, but they were muffled by the howling wind. When the plane approached the island, I could see beautiful blue water and small whitecaps that dotted the open sea. But in my heart and in my vision, I knew it was simply veneer and what lay under the veneer was a version of hell.

The line at customs and immigration was short as so many people were concerned about the potential for Dennis and Ellen to hit the island.

"Where will you be staying?" the customs agent asked.

"Let me check." I couldn't remember. I looked

at the reservation form. "I'm staying at the Pelican Hotel." She glanced at the immigration form that I filled out during my flight and verified that I was staying there. She then handed me my passport and stamped the customs form.

"Do you think we'll get the hurricane?" the agent asked.

"You can count on it. You can take it to the bank." She looked at me, confused, obviously not familiar with the expression. "The only question is whether Ellen will catch Dennis and really whip the island." The agent looked terrified after hearing my prediction.

"God help us if it happens."

"Amen," I replied to the agent.

In the Blink of an Eye

Chapter 24

Hotel California

The taxicab ride from the airport to the hotel took 15 minutes. The atmosphere on the island seemed extraordinarily tense as people prepared to be beaten up by Dennis and Ellen. The taxi pulled up to the Pelican Hotel. I gave the taxi driver a $20 bill for a $10 fare and told him to keep the change.

"Thanks, Mon."

"You're welcome. Be safe."

"You too, Mon."

I walked into the lobby. Things looked surreal. There was a black man at the front desk. He was alone. It was clear that the hotel was empty. "Welcome to the Hotel California" played on a small radio sitting on the registration counter.

"How can I help you?"

"My name is Kenney, Michael Kenney. I have a reservation." I handed him the piece of paper with my confirmation number on it.

"Well, Mr. Kenney, it's you and me."

"What do you mean?"

"You and I and my young son will be the only people staying at the hotel. There are no other guests here, at this point."

"Wow."

He extended his hand. "My name is Crosby and my son's name is ..."

"Wait, let me guess. Reggie." His eyes lit up.

"How would you know that?"

"Lucky guess." He shook his head and handed me the key. The number on the room key was 0303.

"Where is the room located?"

"Third floor facing inland. That's the safest room in a hurricane situation."

"Any chance it has a ceiling fan?"

"Yes."

"Great."

"The fan won't help you. We'll lose power as soon as the storm hits."

"Elevator?"

"Get used to the stairs. The elevator runs on electricity too." We laughed. "Welcome to Hurricane Hell, Mr. Kenney."

"Gee, thanks."

The hallway leading to room 0303 was dark and narrow. It had a distinctive odor; a combination of mildew and powdered carpet cleaner. The room door had a magnetic card lock and I hoped the locking mechanism ran on battery power. The room was small with white tile floors and furniture that looked like it had come from a West Indies estate home. I dropped my bag on the bed and turned on the fan switch. The fan didn't move. I tried the next switch and also tried pulling the bead chain on the fan but the blades still didn't move. "Bummer," I thought. Then I opened the sliding glass door to the balcony and a breeze blew across the room. The fan blades started to rotate. I lay down on the bed and stared at the fan. Audrey! I could see a large disk moving through the air. I could hear the sounds of people talking and the clanking of dishes.

Then the phone rang. It was Crosby.

"Mr. Kenney, did you see the weather report?"

"No."

"Ellen is moving south but Dennis is heading right for us. Landfall is expected tomorrow, late afternoon."

"Thanks for the update."

"Ya, Mon. If you want to have dinner, you can

join me and Reggie later on."

"Great, I'd love to."

"How about 6:00?"

"Sounds good. See you then."

I lay back down on the bed: more kitchen noises and more Audrey. Then the phone rang again.

"Mr. Kenney, we have been waiting for you." I looked at my watch. Four hours had elapsed.

"Sorry. I fell asleep. I'll be down in a few minutes." I quickly washed up and walked down to the dining room. "Hello, Reggie."

"How do you know my name?"

"I don't know. You look like a Reggie." Crosby walked into the dining room carrying a bottle of red wine.

"Will you join me in a glass?"

"Sure." We raised our glasses.

"Here's to survival," Crosby announced.

"Cheers." Reggie held up a glass of water and we all toasted.

"Sit down, Mr. Kenney. Dinner will be out in a minute."

"Thanks." The glass of wine went down easy so I poured myself another. After I had taken a sip, I walked over to the hostess desk and noticed a collage of pictures that were displayed on a bulletin board. The pictures were of guests eating and drinking in the restaurant. One picture caught my attention so I took it off the bulletin board and studied it.

"You see someone you know, Mr. Kenney?"

"Who is this girl in this picture?" I pointed to the back of a waitress carrying a large serving tray.

"She's an American."

"Do you know her name?"

"No, I don't remember her name but she always wore a green shirt with yellow letters on it."

"What were the letters?"

"It was either an M and a W or a W and an M."

William and Mary, I thought. "Was her name Audrey?"

"Yeah, that was it, Audrey. Do you know her, Mr. Kenney? She was a real good looker." I didn't answer his question.

"Do you know where she may be?" I asked.

He grabbed the picture from my hand and turned it over. The date was August 1990.

"I haven't seen her in five years. Do you know her?"

"Yeah, I know her, but it's a long story."

Two hours later I was back in my room, half-drunk and watching the local news, which was broadcast in French. Best I could tell, Dennis was a Category 4 storm heading directly for Sint Maarten.

"I guess we're in for the worst storm in a century."

In the Blink of an Eye

Chapter 25

Dennis

At 9 a.m. I woke up to cloudy skies and windy conditions. I walked to the balcony and looked out to see no one. Every once in a while, a gust of wind would ignite a minor sandstorm on the beach that would send small shells airborne, hitting the windward windows of the hotel. I got dressed and walked down to the lobby. Crosby was standing there looking out at the beach. The waves had built to 8 to 10 feet and were beginning to erode the beach.

"Good morning, Crosby."

"Mr. Kenney, how did you sleep?"

"Fine, thanks."

In the Blink of an Eye

"It looks like we're going to take a beating today."

"What is the weather forecast?" I asked.

"Same as yesterday. By three o'clock the eye should be on us. How about some coffee while we still have electric power?"

"Sure." Crosby disappeared into the kitchen as I took his position standing at the lobby entrance.

The wind speed was increasing and the sound of howling winds became more frequent. Then a huge gust occurred and with that, a large piece of sheet metal blew across the beach. I looked down the shore line to see the roof of the chair rental hut was gone. Crosby reappeared. "We lost the roof on the rental hut."

"I'm not surprised," Crosby replied. For the next few hours we sat in the lobby watching the storm. By noon a line appeared in the sky.

"I think that's the eye," Crosby muttered. The eye of the storm looked surreal. It was something that neither of us had seen before.

"I wish the hotel was boarded up," Crosby said.

"Why isn't it?"

"Supplies are scarce on the island."

"Does the owner have insurance?" I asked.

"So he says."

Seconds later, the rain started to pound the hotel. Minutes later, leaks started to appear in the lobby. Crosby, Reggie and I began the process of putting buckets under the leaks but there were so many that it seemed fruitless. Then a beach chair from another hotel blew down the beach and flew into the lobby door, cracking a glass.

"We'd better move inside," Crosby said.

"Good idea." We moved into the kitchen but within minutes the electricity was gone, so we walked back into the lobby where there was light. The waves were now 15 to 18 feet and water was starting to approach the hotel. Minutes later, water moved into the entrance and started to infiltrate the door seals.

"How high are we above ground?"

"Three meters or so," Crosby replied.

More water was leaking under the door and started to flow freely into the lobby. Crosby disappeared for a few minutes then returned with several large bags of rice. We placed them against the door to slow the water.

"We better get upstairs."

Crosby opened a room on the second floor. "Let's try to ride it out here."

The wind continued to howl as we watched the storm. The smaller buildings around us started to disintegrate, as their roofs, windows and doors were ripped from the structure. Debris repeatedly flew into the hotel. Several windows on the first floor shattered from the impact. The lobby was

In the Blink of an Eye

now flooding as the storm surge drove water inland. All the streets around us were flooded as well. The wind gusts and related noise continued to build until it was impossible to hold a conversation.

More leaks began to show. We entered the stairwell and walked to the top floor. Water was pouring in and running down the walls to the lower floors. Sections of the roof flew off the building and the situation was beginning to look dreadful. We returned to the second floor. By now Reggie was terrified and was crying. Crosby held him on his lap and hugged him but was unsuccessful in comforting him. Dennis continued to raise hell for another hour and then all of a sudden, the winds died. We went back to the lobby, wading through a foot of water.

"Look," Reggie shouted. "The sun. The hurricane is over."

"I don't think so. We are in the eye. My guess is that we have about a half an hour before it starts up again.

"Let's survey the damage," Crosby said. We walked the floors of the Pelican Hotel. Ten percent of the windows were blown out on the ocean side. The land side looked fine. The number of leaks was in the hundreds and the smell of mildew started to build. "Not bad," Crosby said.

"I guess it could have been worse." Then just like that, the sky darkened and we were back in

Dennis

Dennis's fury. As the back side of the hurricane hit, the storm surge slowed and the beach began to reveal itself. And while the wind speed appeared to be lessening, the breaking glass and the leaks continued.

As darkness fell, the storm continued to weaken and by 10 p.m. the winds had died down to 20 to 30 knots. The island was now in total darkness and not a single person was seen on the streets. At 11 p.m. Crosby disappeared for a few minutes and returned with a bottle of rum and two glasses.

"I guess we should celebrate. We survived Dennis." By midnight the bottle was gone and so were Crosby and I.

As I slept in my drunken state, the dream sounds started. All night long I heard "Salt, salt, salt, salt, salt ..."

In the Blink of an Eye

Chapter 26

The Veneer of Civility

The sun beaming in through the windows eventually turned room 0205 into a sauna. Reggie woke up first and within a few minutes, I was awake. I had the worst hangover of my life brought on by the cheap rum Crosby and I polished off eight hours earlier. I also had severe dry mouth, created either by the dehydration of drunkenness or by the salt I dreamt about all night. Why salt? How did salt play into my future?

I left the room and walked to room 0303 where my single bag of possessions lay. The hallways were wet and began to smell moldy. I went to each end of the hallway and opened the windows. A refresh-

In the Blink of an Eye

ing breeze blew down the hall.

My room had survived the hurricane and my bag was still lying on the bed. It was wet from the leaks from the fourth, fifth and sixth floors. I emptied the contents on the desk and was fortunate to find some dry underwear. The plumbing, electricity and all of the utilities were nonfunctioning so I decided to walk down to the beach and rinse off in the ocean, which was still as the Chesapeake Bay on a hot August morning.

Crosby walked over to me with three bottles of water.

"Mr. Kenney, you better hydrate."

"Thanks. You're a good man, Crosby. Hey, by the way, do you have a car or truck I can use for an hour or so?"

"I don't think the roads will be passable."

"You're probably right. I think I'll take a walk into town."

"Be careful. Disasters like this don't always bring out the best in people."

"Thanks, good advice." With one bottle down and two bottles of water in my pockets, I started to walk into town. That's when I realized just how devastated the island was. The houses that sat along the road were gone. People sat on the ground in front of their destroyed houses looking into space. They looked like zombies, totally possessed by despair and disbelief.

The Veneer of Civility

As I walked further into town I saw the beginnings of the collapse of civility. People were scavenging for anything they could find. People were looting and the veneer of civility was peeling away from what otherwise was a little piece of paradise. The further I walked into town, the worse it got. Two large teenage boys watched me walk past them and I felt like I was being stalked by two tigers. They got up and started to walk behind me, each step getting them closer and closer. Fear started to overcome me, so I stopped and turned around, finding them three paces behind me. I reached into my pocket and pulled out the two bottles of water and offered it to them. They grabbed them out of my hands, mumbled something in French which I imagined was derogatory and walked away. I continued to walk until I had seen enough devastation. I needed to figure out a way to help these people. I walked back to the hotel.

Crosby and a few others who worked at the hotel were cleaning up the lobby.

"Crosby, can you drive me to the airport in Philipsburg?"

"Sure, if the roads are open."

"Let's try." The drive to the airport was challenging and the closest I could get was within one mile. "I'll be back by day's end or by tomorrow at the latest."

"Where are you going?"

In the Blink of an Eye

"I need to see a man about supplies."

Three hours later I was on my way to Grenada, on a chartered Short 30 aircraft. The charter fee for plane and pilot was $3,000. It was money well spent. Grenada was far enough to the south to have been spared by Hurricane Dennis. The flight took just over an hour. Our mission was to fill the plane with as much water, food and supplies as possible and to immediately return to Sint Maarten.

By day's end, we had cleared customs in and out, purchased pallets of water, bread, fruit and vegetables, and were airborne back to Sint Maarten. Once back, I convinced a truck driver at the airport to help me to deliver the supplies to the hotel where we could help the locals. The customs officer at the airport looked the other way for $250. More money well spent. By the time we left the airport, it was getting dark. When we arrived at the hotel, we met Crosby and unloaded the supplies. Total cost of the plane, the food and the payoffs: about $5,000. "Good investment," I thought.

According to Crosby it would take a week or so to get power back, which meant all the food in the hotel freezers needed to be distributed.

"Crosby, let me buy the food from the hotel. We will set up some barbecues on the beach, cook it up and feed the locals."

"Are you sure, Mr. Kenney?"

"Very sure."

The Veneer of Civility

That night I slept in room 0303 on a semi-dry mattress. At 3 a.m. the moon had risen and began to cast light throughout the room. The breeze from the ocean was sufficient to move the paddles on the ceiling fan. Seconds later, I was in a trance staring at the fan blades and blinking my eyes. It was Audrey again, walking on a debris-filled road. She passed a sign, Grand Case. Then I saw a restaurant on the waterfront with green shutters. Audrey walked up the street and disappeared. My future was getting closer.

I stayed up most of the night trying to invoke more images but was unsuccessful. By 6 a.m. I had fallen asleep again and went into dream sound mode. I could hear Audrey's voice. "Michael, what are you doing here? How did you get here?" Then a man's voice. "Nice to meet you, Michael. I have lost my sons." Then Audrey's voice again. "Why are you testing me? Didn't you read my poem?" Then "Salt, salt, salt, salt ..."

In the Blink of an Eye

Chapter 27

Grand Case

The next two days were beautiful from a weather viewpoint. But from a humanity viewpoint, things still looked grim. All the looting had stopped as there was nothing left to loot. People started to look after each other and the angry faces that I had experienced two days earlier were turning to occasional smiles. The makeshift beach barbecues were working out fine as we helped to bridge the hunger gap. The locals were clearly grateful for the assistance and I was happy to have helped. That afternoon as we continued the cleanup, I asked Crosby about the use of his truck.

"Where are you going, Mr. Kenney?"

In the Blink of an Eye

"I would like to drive over to Grand Case."

"What for?"

"I have a friend I want to see."

"Who, the waitress?"

"Yeah."

"How do you know she's there?"

"I don't know. I just have a hunch."

"How did you know my son's name? Was that a hunch, too? Mr. Kenney, do you see the future?"

"Crosby, let's hold that for another day." He flipped me his keys to his truck.

"Why don't you take some water with you?"

"Good idea."

So began my journey to Grand Case, located on the French side of the island. According to Crosby, the trip should have taken 45 minutes but in the post-Dennis Sint Maarten, it could take days.

"You have to go over the mountains to get there. Be careful. Some of the roads may be washed out."

"Thanks, Crosby."

The trip out of town seemed to take forever. Every street was littered with debris. There were abandoned cars that were turned over by the wind and the floods. Some cars were stripped, others had been left alone. There was dead livestock on the road's edge. Several dead dogs were being picked apart by birds and the smell of death was overwhelming. One hour into the trip, I had made

Grand Case

only 10 miles of progress. This was partly due from having to stop to move tree limbs out of the road and partly because I had stopped several times to give water to some people who looked like they hadn't had a drink in days.

The interior of the island looked worse than the coast, mostly due to the downed trees and power lines that ran along the roadside. After four hours of driving, I finally got to Grand Case. The town, like every other village I went through, looked devastated. Many of the beachfront restaurants were totally gone and the remainder were damaged. I parked the truck next to the police station and walked to the beach in search of the green restaurant building that I had seen in my flashes. At the far end of town and along the beach, I could see what was left of the green building. It, like so many others, had taken a beating from Dennis. The long stretch of damaged buildings looked like a building graveyard.

As I approached what was left of the green building, I found a canoe oar lying on the beach. The oar was green and on it was painted the words, "The Greenhouse Beach Bar." I took the oar and placed it next to the building. Then, I walked back toward the street that paralleled the beach. Many of the houses were made from cement block and actually looked pretty good compared to the houses I had seen earlier. At the end of the street, I

In the Blink of an Eye

turned right onto another street and stopped. My heart started racing. A lump grew in my throat. I was frozen in time. There stood Audrey, just like in the flashes.

A little girl stood next to her. The house they were standing in front of had been destroyed. I tried to move but I couldn't. "Michael," I said to myself, "this is the way it's supposed to happen." I continued to walk toward her, my mind still replaying everything I saw in the flashes. She looked down the street at me and did a double take. I continued to walk toward her. My heart was on fire. "Okay, she will say, 'Michael what are you doing here? How did you get here?'" Now she had her hand over her mouth. Then she leaned down to the girl and whispered something. The girl ran away. I continued to walk toward her. I finally stopped four feet in front of her. We stared at each other for a split second.

"Michael, what are you doing here? How did you get here?"

"Hello, Audrey. I hope I haven't …" She cut me off in mid-sentence.

"I hope you didn't think you could just walk into my life after all this time?"

"Audrey, I don't know what to think."

"Why are you testing me? Didn't you read my poem?"

"Yes I did, though it took several months for

me to get it." She started to calm down.

I looked over her shoulder at the destroyed house. "Was that your house?"

"No, it belongs to a friend of mine. She's in the hospital. That was her daughter who we are watching."

"We?"

"Yes, I live with my fiancé."

"Oh, I see." My heart started to break. She reached for my hand. I felt a shock run up my arm.

"Michael, you broke my heart. I loved you so much, for so long, but you just couldn't see that."

"Audrey, the only thing I can say is I'm sorry and I'm not here to interfere with your life. Maybe I should go."

"No." Our hands were still locked together. She started walking toward the beach.

"Where are we going?"

"I don't know."

We walked along the beach for what seemed like a mile. We didn't talk. Audrey simply looked ahead, her mind thinking about what had just happened. Then she stopped and faced me. She took her hand and ran it through my hair. Our eyes were locked on each other, then our eyes closed and our lips touched. My heart pounded as the kiss matured. I felt more in love with Audrey than I ever had before. The problem was that it was not mutual. As the kiss ended, so did any lingering feelings that Audrey may have had for me.

"Michael, thank you. I needed that."

"Needed what, to confirm that you have no feelings for me?"

"I wouldn't say that, but I would say that I know there is someone who has mended my broken heart." I said nothing.

We turned and retraced our steps back to her house, our hands still locked together. "So Audrey, I guess I should go."

"You don't have to if you would like to stay …"

This time I cut her off in mid-sentence.

"Look, I need to move on. You've seemed to have done that and it would be better for both of us if I go. But before I do, I want to answer a few questions you have asked. First, let me tell you why I came to Sint Maarten and how I found you. Then I will tell you all that I know about Angel."

"Angel from the plantation?"

"Yes, Angel Lehcar."

We sat on the porch on separate chairs that were divided by a small table. Two large palm trees shaded the powder blue cement block house.

"By the way, what does your fiancé do?"

"He works for the power company."

"He must be busy."

"He has been working 24/7. He hasn't been

home since the hurricane hit and won't be home for a few more days."

Thoughts started to run through my mind but I was quick to shut them down.

"First, let me tell you why I am in Sint Maarten and how I got here."

I started from the beginning, taking her all the way back to Jost, Sonnet, Janet Jones, and Radcliffe Brown. I told her all about Angel Lehcar and explained that Angel wasn't calling out to me, "Michael," as we both thought but rather was chanting "My kill." I told her about the cemetery and the thunderstorm and about the images I had seen about the future. All she could say was, "I knew it, I knew it, I knew it."

"So Audrey, as much as I wanted to let you in, I just couldn't. I'm so sorry."

She stood up. "Come inside for a minute." We walked into the living room and she shut the door behind me.

"Michael, I hope I don't live to regret this."

Our eyes closed; our lips touched. The kiss went on and on. And when it finally ended, I knew she was back in touch with the feelings she once had for me.

She walked away and sat on a chair in the corner of the room. Her hands covered her eyes and I could see tears rolling down her cheeks. She said nothing. She was unable to speak.

In the Blink of an Eye

"Audrey, are you okay? Did we do the wrong thing?" She raised her hand and pointed toward the door, gesturing me to leave.

Like a fool, I complied with her wish. That was the last time I saw or heard from Audrey.

That night I arrived at the hotel with no memory of how I got there. Crosby was in the lobby when I returned.

"Mr. Kenney, how did it go?"

"Crosby, I may have made a huge mistake."

"What happened?"

"I'll tell you in the morning." I went back to room 0303 and took out a sheet of paper from the desk.

Dear Crosby,

It's time for me to go. Thank you for everything. You are truly a remarkable man. I have left for you a small packet of sand as a way for you to remember my time in Sint Maarten and the friendship we created. The sand came from a Buddhist sand mandala. It holds the secret to inner peace. Remember that the key to feeling peace within can only be realized when you allow your life to be guided by both wisdom and compassion. Have a wonderful life. My love to Reggie.

Sincerely,
Michael

Grand Case

At 4 a.m. I walked down to the lobby and stood behind the registration counter. I folded the letter in thirds, sealed it with a single staple, and left it at the registration desk. I walked out into the early morning air and started to walk to the airport. I never returned to Sint Maarten again.

In the Blink of an Eye

Chapter 28

Bad Findings

If you showed me 100 buildings and one of them was a hospital and 99 were anything else, I assure you I could pick out the hospital. Hospitals can best be described as a really bad hotel design. Take a hotel, add a certain smell, a cafeteria, and some technology and what you have is a hospital. There is one other difference; most guests do not get bad news when they stay in a hotel.

I was a bit on edge as I drove through the Hampton Roads Bridge Tunnel toward Norfolk. I was going to the same facility that tended to Anne Kenney and me at the time of our separation. I tried not to focus on Anne and I tried not to re-

In the Blink of an Eye

member the sound of the monitors beeping and the voices of the doctors and the sound of the respirator switch being turned off. But somehow I was obsessing on my mother's death.

The halls in the hospital were long. The white tile floors, white painted walls and the endless fluorescent lights made me feel like I was in an insane asylum. For all I knew, maybe I was. I finally came to a turn in the hallway and spotted the sign I was looking for: Neurosciences Division -- Dr. Ti Kim. "Nice name for a doctor," I thought. The waiting room was empty of people and warmth. It seemed to be an artistic replica of a hospital hallway.

I approached the reception window.

"Please sign in,'" the receptionist said. "Your name, please?"

"Michael Kenney."

"Insurance card?"

"Sure."

"Thanks, Mr. Kenney. Please fill out this questionnaire and bring it back to me when you're done."

"Okay, thanks." I sat down and filled out the basics. Then I came to the family history section.

-Do you have any living parents?

No, died in an accident. I skipped the explanation.

-Do you have any siblings?

Bad Findings

Yes.

-How many?

One (I lied.).

-If yes is/are he or she still living?

No.

-If no, what was the cause of death?

Brain tumor. Then the questions turned to me.

-Do you have high blood pressure?

No.

- Do you have headaches?

Yes, occasionally.

-Any loss of memory?

Yes.

Then I turned the page over and looked at the next thirty questions. I answered no to all of them.

I signed the form and handed it to the receptionist. "Thanks. Dr. Kim will be with you in a few minutes. Come through the door, and I'll walk you to the exam room."

"Thanks."

We walked down the hall and into a small 10 feet by 10 feet white box.

"Strip down to your underwear and take a seat at the end of the exam table. Dr. Kim will be right in."

"Thanks." Ten minutes later, Dr. Kim entered

In the Blink of an Eye

the room. He was rather young, very tall and spoke with a Canadian accent.

"Hello, Mr. Kenney." He extended his hand.

"Nice to meet you, Dr. Kim." He sat next to me and began to review the questionnaire.

"Mr. Kenney, tell me about your brother's brain tumor."

"Well, I don't know much. He died when I was a baby (another lie.)

"How old was he?

"About 40 years old."

"Your brother was 40 years older than you."

"Not exactly."

"Do you want to explain this to me?"

"No."

"How old were your parents when they died?"

"They were in their 30s."

"Mr. Kenney, this doesn't make any sense."

"Dr. Kim, what are you?

"I'm a neurologist."

"I mean about your faith. What are you, Christian, Buddhist or what?"

"Buddhist."

"Okay that helps. My brother is my pre-incarnate."

"Your pre-incarnate?"

"Yes. The person I was reincarnated from, died of a brain tumor."

"So Mr. Kenney, do you have a brother at all?"

Bad Findings

"No."

"Okay, good. Tell me about your pre-incarnate."

"It's going to take a while."

"I'm all ears."

I started from the beginning and ended it with Sonnet's death. I didn't mention anything about Angel or the future.

"Wow, Mr. Kenney. Unbelievable."

"Tell me about it."

"So your major issue is memory loss."

"Yes, just like Jost."

"Let's do some basic diagnostics."

"Okay."

For the next hour, I was poked and prodded, made to stand on one leg at a time, and read sentences forward and backward. He checked my balance, my vision, my hearing, and everything else other than my reproductive organ and colon.

"Mr. Kenney, you seem to be in good health. I would like to order some blood work and an MRI. My nurse will come in and draw your blood and I'm going to see if I can get you in for the MRI right now."

"Great."

"By the way, are you claustrophobic?"

"I don't think so."

"Good. Get dressed and relax. I'll be back in a few minutes."

In the Blink of an Eye

Twenty minutes later my blood was drawn and I was being escorted to radiology. The MRI resembled a tubular coffin. Just the sight of it made me a bit claustrophobic and paranoid. The nurse could see my facial expression.

"Mr. Kenney, I can give you a sedative if you're feeling anxious."

"No, I'll be okay."

"All right. Lie down on the table. We are going to slide you in. The test will take about 45 minutes. You may be more comfortable if you keep your eyes closed."

"Good advice," I thought to myself. Then the table moved gently as I was maneuvered into the tube.

"Are you okay?"

"Yes." I closed my eyes and started to dream. The voices started. "Mr. Kenney, I'm sorry, salt, salt, welcome." Then I could hear Su crying. I opened my eyes. My face was within eight inches from the upper side of the tube. I closed my eyes again and fell back asleep. The sounds came back. "Stars, stars." Then the sound of sails luffing. "Salt, salt, welcome, welcome."

The sound of the MRI was so loud, I couldn't fall asleep again. Then the gantry moved and I was on my way out. The nurse from Dr. Kim's office was waiting outside the room.

Bad Findings

"Mr. Kenney, what is your schedule?"

"I have no schedule."

"If you want to come back in about two hours, Dr. Kim should have read the study and will be able to share the results with you."

"Fine, I'll come back in two hours." I decided to drive to Willoughby Harbor Marina to check out the boats, hoping it would distract me from my concern, but all I could do was think of the words "Mr. Kenney, I'm sorry."

At 2 p.m. I returned to Dr. Kim's office.

"Mr. Kenney, the doctor will see you now." The nurse walked me down the hall and into his office. Dr. Kim stood up as I walked in.

"Mr. Kenney, sit down. I studied your MRI and also had several of my colleagues review the study as well." He paused and took a deep breath. "Mr. Kenney, I'm sorry. The MRI revealed some issue of great concern." I was speechless. "There's a small tumor in the deep brain. It's likely that it is affecting your memory. The good news is that it is a slow-growing tumor and is not likely cancerous."

"What exactly does that mean?"

"You could have three years, or you could have 10 years. We don't really know."

"Can it be removed?"

"No, it's way too deep inside the brain."

"What about radiation?"

"Radiation is not really an option."

In the Blink of an Eye

"What can I expect for quality-of-life?"

"No pain, increasing memory loss, eventually dementia and a quiet end. I do recommend that you get a second opinion."

"I'll do that."

"Mr. Kenney, I'm so sorry, I really am."

"Thanks, Doc."

Two weeks later I flew to the New York to the Center of Neurosciences. I met with three physicians, each the best in their field: a neurologist, neurosurgeon and radiation oncologist. They simply confirmed Dr. Kim's finding.

Chapter 29

Stones

Denial is an odd state of mind. Refusal to accept fact is truly a human emotion. After several days of denial I moved to acceptance. However, with acceptance came a several-day pity party. No one was invited. I partied alone. I spent several hours wondering if things would have been different with my meeting with Audrey if I knew of my condition and had told her. I contemplated calling her but decided against it. I figured I'd already done enough damage. I needed to tell Su and Allen, Paul Curry and Jodii. I also needed to talk to Mick Dermott so he could update my will.

Several days later, I went home to be with my

In the Blink of an Eye

parents. I already knew Su's reaction as I had heard her crying hysterically in my dreams. Allen's reaction was surprising. When I told him, he walked away and went outside. I didn't follow him. I stayed to comfort Su. When Allen returned, I could tell he was unable to cope. He looked like he was aging in place. Finally he said something about his vision for our future and that his dream would have to be accelerated. I didn't ask what his dream was about.

Paul was a mess and was also showing signs of denial but finally accepted the truth. Jodii, on the other hand, was calm. This was predictable. We meditated together and his presence gave me strength. He said a great opportunity had been given to me and now I needed to live life to the fullest and to prepare for the next reincarnation. He told me to meditate focusing on the future and that a vision of my reincarnation would come to me. As I left the temple, I slipped him an envelope. It was money well spent.

The church which oversaw the cemetery where Jost and Angel was buried was old and in some level of disrepair. I wasn't in the habit of going to a Catholic church but I had some business to take care of. The church had a musty smell, a sign of insufficient investment in the air-conditioning system. There were speakers attached to the wall above the altar, which looked out of place. I walked to the altar and lit a candle for Anne and Stephen Kenney, Jost, Sonnet, and Angel. Then I lit another candle for Audrey. I could feel the presence of someone behind me, so I turned around to find a young priest standing there. "Are you Father Delao?"

"Yes. Are you Mr. Kenney?"

"Yes, but please call me Michael."

"I will if you call me Michael."

"I see our parents showed great wisdom in the selection of our names."

"Yes they did," the priest said. "So Michael Kenney, what can I do for you?"

"I want to make a sizable donation to your church."

"That's something I rarely hear. Are you a member of the church?"

"No, in fact I am not Catholic nor even Christian."

"What are you?"

"Hebrew and Buddhist."

"You're a Bujew."

"Exactly."

"Interesting mixture. So why this church? Is there a hitch?"

"Yes, there is."

"What is it?"

"Father, I want to replace a stone for two people

who are buried in your cemetery."

"Why?"

"You don't get to ask that question."

"What else, Mr. Kenney?"

"I want to be buried next to the tombstones I plan to replace."

"What else?"

"I want to take the stone of the two individuals who will be getting the new stones."

"Michael, are you implying that two people are sharing one stone?"

"Yes, that's correct."

"Interesting. Walk with me."

We walked out to the cemetery. "You know, Michael, I rarely come out here. No one has been buried here for a long time."

"I know." We walked to Jost and Angel's stone. "Father, looked at this." I showed him the upside-down engraving of Angel Lehcar and engraving on the other side that said Jost Alexson. Father Delao kneeled down.

"Michael, look at this."

"What?"

"Jost's name was engraved over another name." I examined the stone.

"You're right. Can you tell what it says?"

"Looks like . . ."

"Let me guess. Angel Lehcar?"

"Yes, I think so."

Stones

"Amazing."

"Michael, let me get this straight. You want to be buried next to his grave, using the old stone for yourself and you want to replace that stone with two new ones."

"Yes, that's correct, one stone for Jost and one for Angel."

"Michael, I have one more question."

"What, Father?"

"Do either Jost or Angel have living relatives?"

"No."

"Are you sure?"

"Yes for Jost and Angel, I think not."

"And the level of the gift you are considering?"

"How about twenty thousand?"

"And you will cover the cost of the new stone?"

"Yes."

"Okay, I accept your donation."

"And Father, this stays between us?"

"That is correct, Michael."

So we shook hands and agreed to work out the details over the next week. Father Delao walked back to the church. I stayed and sat next to the stone.

"So Jost, tell me how it came to be that you shared a stone with Angel." There was no reply.

In the Blink of an Eye

Chapter 30

SALT

Everyone, including me, seemed to be coming to grips with my brain tumor, with one exception. Mick Dermott wasn't taking the news well. I think he felt a bit guilty, as if he had made some special commitment to Anne and Stephen Kenney, a commitment which he was no longer able to keep. Mick Dermott was also bothered by my unwillingness to name the beneficiary in my will. Every time he broached the topic I would tell him that my life was to take some interesting twists and that those twists and turns might impact where my assets would land.

I was still hearing sounds in the night as I

In the Blink of an Eye

dreamed: welcome, salt, David, Robert, sounds of motors running at high speed, voices of people saying stars and voices calling out names that resembled Greek gods and goddesses.

I decided to treat myself to a new computer. I purchased the very best I could find and had the local cable company install a high-speed Internet connection. I began the process of trying to put together a series of searches with the hopes that somehow I would get a look into the future. I spent several days online until I began to realize that only one word held the key to the future.

The word "salt" linked almost all the others together. Salt was not the square crystal used to season our food. Nor did it have anything to do with the oceans. Salt simply meant Southern African Large Telescope. It made perfect sense; stars, constellations, and the sound of motors moving the large telescope. As to Robert and David, I had no clue. All I knew was that somehow I would find myself in South Africa. The question not yet answered was when. Rather than push the issue, I decided to wait for another sign. In the meantime, life went on as usual as if the tumor didn't exist.

The bouts of forgetfulness seemed to have stabilized. The episodes always seemed to manifest themselves in the same manner. I would forget names, places, where I put things and occasionally, I couldn't remember why I was at a specific place.

SALT

When that happened, I would pull out my schedule in my pocket. The daily schedule was the best tool for remembering the issues of the day.

The friendship I had with Paul Curry, while still a very important part of my life, was different now. I didn't know if it was related to my terminal illness or something else. It seemed like he was keeping something from me or that he had a secret he wanted to tell me, but couldn't. So often I would find myself asking him if something was bothering him or if he needed to get something off his chest. He only said that everything was fine and not to worry.

There were some new images coming into view as I continued my ceiling fan addiction. I started to see images of a man sitting in a restaurant. The restaurant was very upscale. I could see him talking to me. He looked stressed as if a terrible thing had happened to him. Then I would see an image of a girl that I had seen before, many years earlier. She too was in the same restaurant but not in the presence of the other man. There were images of sailing in the open ocean on a large sloop. Allen was on board. There were many islands in view and I wondered if this was going to present an opportunity to see Audrey again. And while it would have seemed quite appropriate to ask Allen if he had any idea about sailing in the islands, I wanted to let things develop on their own.

In the Blink of an Eye

Then events started to unfold. First, I got a phone call from Jodii. That was a very unusual occurrence. In fact, it was the first time he had ever called me.

"Hello."

"Hello, Michael."

"Jodii, is that you?"

"Yes, my friend."

"Is everything okay?"

"Yes, all is well. I have an opportunity for you."

"You have my attention."

"How would you like to come on a trip with me?"

"What type of trip?"

"I have an opportunity to lecture at a university in Africa."

"Are you talking South Africa?"

"Yes, how did you know?"

"I saw it in a flash."

"The trip will also take us to some interesting places and to some interesting meetings."

"What kind of meetings?"

"We have been invited to a meeting where a scientist will be discussing a project to develop a new telescope in South Africa."

"Is it SALT, the Southern African Large Telescope?"

"Yes, Michael, correct again."

SALT

"When are we leaving?"

"Not so fast. I have a favor to ask of you. I want you to speak at the lecture about the Bujew."

"Me? You're kidding?"

"No jokes from me. Will you do it?"

"Yes, absolutely."

"We are leaving in 90 days. You need to start preparing your lecture and you'll need to pay for your travel expenses."

"No problem. Jodii, does the word Rubin or Rubeen have any meaning to you?"

"No. What does it mean?"

"I don't know."

"It will come to you soon enough, Michael, I'm sure. I'll call you with travel plans and the meeting agenda."

"Excellent. Jodii, thanks again."

"You're welcome. Keep up the meditation."

"You too."

I hung up the phone and walked over to the computer. "Here comes the future," I said to myself. I opened up the search engine and typed in Cape Town + Rubin. No hits came back. Then I tried Cape Town + Rubeen. But still there were no hits. So I pulled out my journal where I had been recording my image flashes and dream sounds and started to cross off all the items that had to this point, been unresolved. The list of unresolved issues was small. Still unresolved were David, Robert,

In the Blink of an Eye

the man in the restaurant, the girl in the restaurant
and sailing in the islands.

Chapter 31

Being Remembered

I had been thinking about what I would put on my stone. I was also trying to think about what I might put on the stones for Jost and Angel. After roaming through some of the local cemeteries, I came to realize that most stones are inscribed very simply: name, birth date, death date. Some stones address how the deceased may have served his country. Some stones have religious symbols engraved on them: a crucifix or Star of David. There were no official symbols for the Bujew.

The man I spoke to at the stone engraving business had very little to offer in the way of suggestions as to what should, or should not, be said on a person's stone. I decided to consult Jodii. He also had very little to offer, so I took it upon myself to deal with the matter.

> *Angel Lehcar, a woman, a slave and a mother, who was raped and who took revenge upon her rapist. Who was hung by order of the Judge of Elizabeth City Courts and whose soul was taken to Heaven. Who was reincarnated into others, and eventually reincarnated into Jost Alexson, who was later reincarnated into Michael Kenney, whose remains lie next to Angel.*

> *Jost Alexson, brother to Sonnet Alexson and father to Emily Jones. Who immigrated from Sweden, who was a craftsman and legendary racer, who died from a brain tumor and who was reincarnated from Angel Lehcar and others and was reincarnated into Michael Kenney whose remains lie next to Jost.*

And on my stone will be my name, date of birth and date of death. This was spelled out in my will.

The engraver read aloud the stone engraving instructions, shook his head and asked if I was sure I wanted all this detail on the stones of two people who were already deceased.

"Look, if the job is too tough, I'm sure I can find another engraver."

Being Remembered

"No, no, I'll do it. It's just weird."

"I'll be the judge of weird; you just get the stones done."

"Okay, I'll call you next week to review the layouts."

"Great, and by the way, if you talk to anyone about this, I'll cancel the deal."

"My lips are sealed."

"Good."

Two weeks later, the layouts arrived by U.S. mail. The new stones would be about 4 feet tall. My stone, the one once shared by Angel and Jost, was about 2 feet tall. I stopped by the church and had Father Delao review the layouts. He gave me his blessing and the deeds for the three plots. I gave him a check for $20,000. It was money well spent.

In the Blink of an Eye

Chapter 32

Cape Town

The 90 days leading up to the South Africa trip sped by. My work preparing for the lecture was complete and it seemed to have resonated with Su, Allen and Jodii. The lecture topic was entitled "Religious Convergence-The Evolution of the Bujew" which explored the meaning and significance of embracing two somewhat conflicting beliefs. One faith has a strong belief in God, while the other faith does not recognize the existence of a supreme being.

The flight to Cape Town was unbelievably long. I tried to offer Jodii first-class accommodation, but he refused, so I sat with him in coach. Like all

In the Blink of an Eye

planes, the seats were narrow and the leg room was minimal. It was just another version of the MRI, except this time my imprisonment was 21 hours rather than 45 minutes. One thing that made the long hours bearable was the flight attendant in our cabin. She was a near carbon copy of Audrey and in some sick way, her presence seemed to torture me. The torture felt good.

The other strange thing was that Audrey had started to appear again in my flashes. I saw her sitting on her couch in the living room. She was on the phone talking to someone. The expression on her face showed great despair. Sometimes she stood up and walked quickly from one end of the room to the other. She paced back and forth. I tried to read her lips but her hand and the phone were always blocking my view. In my dreams I heard nothing associated with the image flashes of Audrey.

I decided to pop a sleeping pill six hours into the trip. Jodii, on the other hand, just meditated the trip away. The sleeping pill did a great job of putting me under; I didn't wake for eight hours. A few hours after I woke we began our descent into Cape Town. The sun was rising over the city and the beauty of the Cape Town harbor was electrifying. It took 90 minutes to go through the process of clearing immigration, retrieving our bags, and clearing customs. We waited a half-hour for a taxi and after

Cape Town

a 45-minute ride, arrived at the Cape Town Resort and Conference Center, which looked out on the harbor.

I approached the registration desk. "How can I help you?" the registration clerk asked.

"I have two rooms in the name of Kenney."

"Welcome to Cape Town, Mr. Kenney." She glanced over at Jodii as if she'd never seen a Buddhist monk before. She looked curiously at the robe he was wearing. "Both rooms are on the sixth floor with the view of the harbor."

"Thanks." We continued the process, got our keys and walked to the concierge desk.

"How can I help you?"

"Where do you recommend for dinner?" He glanced at Jodii in the same way the registration clerk did and then handed me a 3-inch binder.

"You'll find all the local restaurants in here, as well as sample menus."

"Thanks."

"Let me know if you need a reservation."

"Okay." Jodii had walked to the lobby restrooms so I took the book and started flipping through it. The restaurants were listed in alphabetical order. When I got to the "R's," there it was: Reubens. I walked back to the concierge. "Excuse me, where is Reubens?"

"Reubens is directly across the street from the

In the Blink of an Eye

hotel." He walked out from behind the concierge stand and pointed to a sign that was fully visible from the lobby. "Fabulous restaurant, though pricey," he said.

"Are they open for lunch?"

"No, they open at 4 p.m., with the first reservation at 5 p.m. Can I make a reservation for you?"

"No thanks."

"Another piece of the puzzle solved," I thought to myself. Jodii soon returned, so we picked up our bags and took the elevator to the sixth floor and went to our rooms. "Jodii, I think I'm going to rest for an hour. How about we meet in the lobby at one o'clock for lunch?"

"I'll see you then, Michael."

The room was typical for a conference center hotel. It had a bed, bathroom, couch, and a small coffee machine that sat on the desk, next to the window that overlooked the harbor. There was no ceiling fan. After unpacking I set the alarm for 12:30 and went to sleep. The sounds and words appeared almost instantly: mac, south, England, Robert, David, each word repeating itself over and over.

I woke up to the sound of the alarm and a pounding headache. When I arrived in the lobby, Jodii was waiting.

"How are you, Michael?"

"Exhausted. I'll be right back." I walked to the

concierge desk.

"Do you need a reservation at Reubens?"

"No thanks." I reached into my pocket and pulled out a piece of paper with three words written on it: mac, south, England. "Do any of these words have significance to this area?" He looked at the paper.

"Well, South England Street is just down the harbor."

"Really?"

"Yes, but mac means nothing to me."

"Thanks. By the way, which way is down to the harbor?"

"About 10 blocks past Reubens, then one block toward the sea wall."

"Thanks, my friend."

"Any time."

I walked back to where Jodii was sitting. "Come on. Lunch awaits us." We walked past Reubens and found a small restaurant named Pauleys. We took a seat overlooking the harbor, ordered a couple of salads and drinks and soaked up the sunshine. "Jodii, do you want to take a short walk after lunch?"

"Sure, Michael."

Lunch was completed in the blink of an eye so we started our walk toward South England Street. "Jodii, keep your eyes out for anything that has the word mac in it."

"Why mac?"

In the Blink of an Eye

"I'm trying to solve a puzzle." South England Street was a short street that ran perpendicular to the harbor. By U.S. standards it would have been called an alley. There were several businesses that called South England Street their home, but none of them looked particularly prosperous. As we approached the end of the street, Jodii pointed to a sign on the building.

"There is your mac word." Attached to the building was a sign: Mac Delivery Service. I walked across the street to the entrance. The door was locked and there was no sign of life inside. The office was abandoned.

"Come on, let's go."

"Michael, why mac?"

"Somehow it is the key to the future." We started our walk back to the hotel. At the entrance of the alley was a postal truck. There was a young man sitting in the vehicle thumbing through the mail.

"Excuse me, do you know what happened to Mac Delivery Service?"

"They moved to the next block."

"Are they still in business?"

"Oh yeah, but who knows for how long."

"Come on Jodii, we have some investigating to do."

One block over was North England Street, which was a carbon copy of South England Street.

Cape Town

I immediately spotted the Mac Delivery Service sign and walked toward the entrance. The door to the office was open, so we walked in. There were two people in the office, both who looked up to see Jodii and me standing there. They, like everyone else, were surprised to see a monk in their establishment.

"Can I help you?"

"Yes. Is Mac here?"

"I'm John Mac."

"John, my name is Michael Kenney. This is Jodii."

"Nice to meet you. So, Mr. Kenney, what can I do for you?"

"Is there somewhere we can talk privately?"

"What about?"

"I'm not sure."

"Connie, give me a minute." Connie walked outside. "Okay, Mr. Kenney, what's on your mind?"

"First tell me about your business."

"Okay, there are two operations here. One is a delivery service. We arrange for boat deliveries from various Cape Town manufacturers to their new owners worldwide. We also operate a small marina at the end of South England Street. So, Mr. Kenney, now it's your turn."

"Well, this may seem strange, but somehow, either I'm here to help you or I'm here for you to help me."

He laughed. "Do you have any money, Mr. Kenney?"

"What is your money issue?"

"Let's see. In U.S. dollars, maybe $100,000."

"What do you need it for?"

"I have a loan on the business. My house is collateralizing the loan. If I can't refinance the loan, I lose my house."

"Why can't you refinance it?"

"I refinanced it already and we are in an economic downturn."

"What do I get if I pay off the loan?"

"I'll give you the business as long as you are willing to employ me and my staff."

"Does the business produce enough cash to pay the operating expenses?"

"Yes."

"Do you have any financial statements I could see?"

"Sure. Are you serious about buying my business?"

"Maybe." Jodii just stood there in amazement. "Look, give me a copy of your financial statements and I'll look them over and get back to you in a few days. Deal?"

"Deal, Mr. Kenney." John went to the photocopier and made two sets of the financial statements, for the last two years. "Here are two copies.

Cape Town

Maybe Monk Jodii would like to study them." I smiled.

We started our walk back to the hotel. Jodii seemed to be mesmerized by the financial statements.

"Jodii, do you know what they say?"

"No, Michael. Do you?"

"I'm probably only slightly more knowledgeable than you. I think I'll fax a copy to Mick Dermott. He'll know how to advise us."

In the Blink of an Eye

Chapter 33

Reubens

I was still feeling exhausted despite having just taken a shower. I had made plans to meet Jodii and a few others for dinner at 8 p.m., but before that I needed to spend some time in Reubens to see if the man in my flash would appear.

Ninety-nine percent of the time I wore either a brown contact lens over my blue eye or blue contact lens over my brown eye. This process had eliminated all the strange looks and weird questions that I had to experience in my early years of growing up. But today was to be different. As I leaned over the sink, I removed the single contact and was reminded of what I had seen in my last

In the Blink of an Eye

flashes. The strange man and I were sitting at the bar chatting. The flashes alternated from his face to my face. And in those flashes of myself I could see my blue eye and brown eye.

At 6 p.m. I walked into the bar at Reubens. Everything felt staged, as if I was entering a set of a movie production. The bar was crowded. The clanking of glasses seemed incredibly loud. There was a rugby match being televised. The volume of the TV was so low that no one could have possibly heard it. I walked to the middle of the bar to get the best vantage point. There was one seat empty out of approximately 30. I took it and looked to my right and to my left. Neither person even remotely looked like a man I was looking for.

"Can I get you a drink?" the bartender asked.

"Sure, I'll have a martini, on the rocks, dry and dirty."

"Right away."

A few minutes later, the drink came. And a few minutes after that, the guy to my right left the bar. No one took the seat. Then I felt a tap on my shoulder. "Excuse me, anyone using this stool?"

"No, help yourself." He sat down and removed his sunglasses. It was him. "Now what?" I thought. Several minutes drifted by, so I decided to initiate the conversation. "So what brings you Reubens?" He looked over at me and did a double take. He noticed my eyes.

Reubens

"Two things brought me here if you must know."

I extended my hand. "I'm Michael." We shook hands.

"My name is Harry. So Michael, you're obviously an American."

"Yes, and you are obviously Scottish."

"Well, actually I am a South African via Scotland." He looked at my eyes again. "So what brings you to Cape Town?"

"I'm a guest lecturer at a local conference."

"What is the subject matter?"

"Spiritual convergence."

"I think I'll stay away from that topic."

"So Harry, you said two things brought you here?"

"Yes, first, I got some bad news today and second, my wife is out of town visiting her cousin in Johannesburg, so I decided to stop here and have a drink and a light dinner before I head home."

"Do you want to tell me about the bad news?"

"It's about my boys."

"Do they have names?"

"Robert and David." No surprise, I thought to myself. "David left Cape Town a few years ago to live in the U.K. Today I found out that Robert is also going to be leaving South Africa after graduation. He too is moving to London. You see, Michael, all my life I had visions of my sons growing

In the Blink of an Eye

up in Cape Town and staying close to the family. I can't believe I have lost both of them. Do you any children, Michael?"

"No, I have no family."

"Sorry. You're missing one of the greatest gifts of life."

"Listen, Harry, have faith in your children. They will come back some day and you'll be together."

"How can you be sure?"

"It is the way of the world. It's meant to be."

"When I tell his sister, she will be devastated as well."

"You have a daughter?"

"Oh yes. She's the baby of the family. She's a real free spirit." He reached into his pocket and pulled out his wallet and then extracted a picture. "Here are my wife, the boys, and my daughter."

"Can I see it?"

"Sure."

I took the picture and held it in a way to eliminate the glare. "When was this picture taken?"

"Last year."

"What is your daughter's name?"

"Jade."

My mind started spinning. It was her, the girl in my flashes. She was older than in the flash image by five years or so. I was sure it was her. "How old is she in this picture?"

Reubens

"She had just turned 16 years old."

I handed the picture back to him and he placed it in his wallet.

"Michael, would excuse me a minute? I need to use the washroom."

"No problem." Harry walked across the barroom and down the hall. I paid my tab and walked out of Reubens.

I had an hour before I needed to meet Jodii and the others. When I got back to the room, I turned on the TV and surfed the channels looking for snow. After 60 channels I found no snow, so I turned the TV around to remove the cable connection. I turned the TV back on. There was snow on every station. I shut off the lights and sat on the bed staring at the television. Then I started to blink. There was Jade sitting at Reubens. She looked older. Her face showed concern and loneliness. Then another flash. This time it was me sitting at the opposite end of the bar. Then another flash. It was a close-up view of my face. I saw my blue and brown eyes. Then she was talking to John Mac. They shook hands.

I closed my eyes for a split second and then started blinking again. This time Jade was different. She was talking to me again. We were on a mountain top and behind her were two harbors, beautiful harbors. I closed my eyes again for a minute. Then I started blinking. This time I didn't

In the Blink of an Eye

like the images I saw. This time she was kneeling at a grave site. I recognized the stone. The name read Michael Kenney.

Chapter 34

A Call from Hampton

I tried to put the idea of death out of my mind, as the level of distraction it caused was remarkable. After all, I knew from Dr. Kim's diagnosis that death was a mere five years out. But actually seeing Jade kneeling at my gravesite gave me such a sick feeling.

The visit to the SALT conference was very stimulating. Scientists from around the world were present to hear about the plans for the new observatory, one that would provide the most spectacular views of the southern sky. In the lobby of the convention center was a micro-scale version of the SALT Observatory. Attendees could operate

In the Blink of an Eye

the dome and mini-telescope by pushing a series of buttons. These buttons engaged small motors that in turn, moved the moving parts of the observatory. The motor noise was familiar to me. It was the sound I heard in my dreams.

The lecture series that Jodi and I were speaking at was just one day away. While I was prepared to deliver my talk, in the back of my mind I was concerned about the possibility of a memory failure. The lecture hall at the university was huge, easily seating 400 people. The room was packed with students and non-students. I was the third lecturer of Day 1 of the conference. Jodii's talk preceded mine. I listened to the first lecturer and then to Jodii. The audience was glued to Jodii and his discussion of the Buddhist way of life.

Right after lunch break it was my turn. The crowd had grown to where people were standing beyond the last row of the auditorium. My anxiety level was peaking as I was introduced by the moderator.

"Good afternoon, it's a real pleasure to be here today to talk about one of my favorite subjects, The Convergence of Faith." And from that moment on, everything flowed. I could see the attendees feverishly taking notes. They were intrigued by the Bujew and the embedded meaning of two faiths that in some ways were complementary and in others ways conflicting. The two-hour lecture sped by

A Call from Hampton

as if I had delivered it in 15 minutes. It ended with a standing ovation, something neither of the two prior lecturers received. It was truly a great day for the Bujews of the world.

At 5 p.m. I returned to my room to find my message light on the phone flashing. I called the message center.

"Michael, this is Mickey. I got your fax. What are you up to? Call me tomorrow to discuss the financial statements for Mac Delivery Service and remember that I am five hours behind you." I decided not to wait until tomorrow and called him immediately.

The phone rang at Mick Dermott's office.

"Edward Dermott's office, how can I help you?"

"This is Michael Kenney. Is Mick Dermott in?"

"Yes, let me transfer you." Mick Dermott picked up the phone.

"Michael, how are you?"

"Great, my lecture is over and went well. So what do you think of the financial statements?"

"Michael, are you really thinking about buying this company?"

"Maybe. So what do you think?"

"There is enough cash flow to pay for operating expenses including the interest expense. You should be able to get a reasonable return on your investment as long as the owners continue to be able to book deliveries. So why do you want to do this?"

"Well, Mick Dermott, it's for personal reasons."

"So what are they?"

"Well first, it is a business I'm interested in. Second, the dollar is strong against the rand. Third, remember what my father wrote in his will. Use the inheritance to improve the world and to help others. This investment would do that."

"Don't you think South Africa is too far away?"

"Yes, it's on the other side of the globe."

"So, why don't you look for an opportunity in the U.S.?"

"Why don't you stop asking questions?"

"I'm a lawyer. It's an occupational hazard. So Michael, what's the real reason?"

"Mick Dermott, I had a dream several weeks ago about this place. It involved John Mac and somehow I need to do this in order for my future to play out as planned."

"As planned by whom?"

"No more questions, Mick Dermott."

"Okay. Tell me what you want me to do."

"I'll call you in a few days or see you when I return to Hampton."

"Okay. Be safe Michael."

A Call from Hampton

"I will."

The next call was to Mac Delivery Service.

"Hello, this is John.

"John, this is Michael Kenney."

"I really didn't expect to hear from you."

"Can I see you tomorrow to discuss the deal?"

"Sure."

"I'll be over at 9 a.m."

"Great."

At 8 a.m. I met Jodii in the lobby, enjoyed a quick breakfast, and walked to Mac Delivery Service. When I arrived, John was sitting at his desk. There was another person sitting at another desk and it was not Connie. I walked in and greeted John. He stood up and walked toward us.

"Michael and Jodii, this is my wife, Sinthis."

"Nice to meet you, Sinthis. I always like a woman with sin in her name." John looked at me as if I had stepped over the line. "Sorry, I once read that line in a book."

"No problem. I asked Sinthis to meet you because she, like me, is curious as to why a stranger would walk into a business that he has no knowledge about and offer to buy the business."

"Does it matter what motivates me?"

"Yes, it matters to us."

"Okay, I'll tell you everything." We walked into a conference room and sat down. "John and Sinthis, do you believe in God?"

227

In the Blink of an Eye

"Yes."

"Do you believe in Heaven and Hell?"

"Yes."

"Can you accept that not everyone shares your belief?"

"I guess so."

"Well, Jodii and I are Buddhists. We believe in reincarnation. Can you accept that?"

"Yes," they both said.

"Great. The next thing you must know is I have a brain tumor and expect to die in the next five to seven years. I also have the ability to see the future through my dreams and meditation. Can you accept that?"

"Maybe."

"John, I had a vision. I've seen a vision of the future that suggest that this business, you and I, and a young woman are somehow tied together. I believe that this girl will work for you, probably as a delivery crew. It is critical that Mac Delivery Service thrives at least until she completes her journey."

"Who is she and when should I expect her?"

"Her name is Jade and she lives somewhere in Cape Town. That's all I know."

Sinthis spoke up. "Mr. Kenney, this is clearly one of the most bizarre stories I've ever heard. On the other hand, I have no reason to doubt your beliefs and besides, we need a way out of this business

A Call from Hampton

loan. John said that he and his crew can continue to work here. Is that true?"

"Yes, all I ask is that you treat this business like it is your own as you have in the past. If we conclude a deal, I will do my best to stay out of your way."

"What will happen to the business when you're gone?"

"What do you mean?"

"When you die?"

"I don't know. Maybe I will give it back to you, who knows?"

"So where do we go from here, Michael?"

"Do you have an attorney here in Cape Town?"

"Yes."

"Give me his name and I will have my attorney call him."

"When do you think we can get this done?" John asked.

"When does the loan come due?"

"In 30 days."

"Then we'll get it done in 29 days."

Sinthis spoke up again. "Mr. Kenney, if you can pull this off, you'll be a saint."

"Sinthis, this is our destiny."

"Jodii, do you have anything to say about this?" I asked.

"I've meditated on this already. It is meant to

be."

"John, I'll call you next week to check on our lawyers' progress."

"Thank you, Michael."

"Glad to be able to help each other."

We walked out of Mac Delivery Service and back to the hotel.

"So Michael, what's next?"

"The beach?"

"What do you mean, beach?"

"Come on, let's rent a car and go to the beach."

"What beach?"

"Scarborough Beach."

"Why there?"

"I heard the name in my dreams."

Chapter 35

Antigua

There was much accomplished in the months that followed my return to Queen Street. I had my follow-up visit with Dr. Kim and as he predicted, the tumor had grown a full centimeter and his prognosis had not changed.

The official currency of South Africa, the rand, had continued to fall in value, so my acquisition of Mac Delivery Service ended up only costing $75,000. I had put new sails on *Sea Pup* and replaced her outboard two-stroke engine with a new four-stroke engine.

My friendship with Paul Curry and Jodii was as strong as ever, although I still felt a strange sense

In the Blink of an Eye

that Paul was hiding something from me.

I also had a few dates, each one failing due to my lack of interest, and my continued need to compare each of them to Audrey.

As for my old Saab Sonett, her engine was rebuilt, new interior installed, and the body repainted. It was money well spent.

Su and Allen had seemed to have forgotten about my illness so everything regarding our relationship seemed normal.

John Mac and I had agreed to a monthly phone call, during which we reviewed delivery contracts and discussed financial results.

I also had taken a few months off from the ceiling fans and the snow. All in all, I felt good about life other than the occasional memory lapse, and the constant longing for Audrey.

I began to spend some time thinking about the end and what I would leave behind as a symbol of my existence and my somewhat complicated life. On the top shelf of my bedroom closet is where I stored all of my journals that I completed from adolescence to now. Each journal was written in a composition notebook. Each notebook had 100 pages, or 200, counting both sides. The journals were full of details and sketches of all my experiences, especially those of Jost, Sonnet and Angel. There were 42 journals in all, including the one I was working on. I estimated that by the time my

Antigua

death occurred I would be up to number 45. So if each journal was to represent a chapter of my life, and each chapter was about 5 pages, then by way of multiplication, I could create an autobiography of 225 pages. It sounded like a reasonable plan. I decided to commit to writing one chapter every two weeks, so in about two years, the book would be ready. However, given the unknown and allowing for procrastination, a more reasonable estimate would say that the book would be completed and ready for distribution in three years.

As the winter season approached, Allen started to talk about a sailing trip in the Caribbean. Allen's idea was that Su, he and I would fly to the Caribbean, pick up a boat and sail for two weeks. His initial suggestion was to depart from Sint Maarten and sail in the Leeward Islands. I, on the other hand, didn't want to get anywhere near Sint Maarten, so I pushed for Antigua. In the end I won. The plan was to sail around Antigua for a few days and then sail on to Guadeloupe, Dominica, Martinique, and then back to Antigua. We all agreed on the itinerary and decided on a Beneteau 473. The date was confirmed for the first week in January, which would not only give us great wind but also great temperatures for sleeping on board the boat.

Three months later on a Friday afternoon, we arrived in English Harbour, Antigua. The boat was

In the Blink of an Eye

very spacious and in good condition for a charter boat. On Saturday we decided to sail over to the west side of the island. We anchored in a small cove and went ashore. Many of the locals encouraged us to go back to English Harbour to experience the party that would take place on Shirley Heights. We decided to experience what the locals suggested. Our first overnight in the harbor was peaceful. Su and I made a simple vegetarian dinner and by nine o'clock we were all fast asleep. The next morning we left the anchorage and sailed toward Montserrat. By noon we reversed course and sailed to Falmouth Harbour. As early evening set in, we went ashore and took a taxi to the party on Shirley Heights. The drive up the mountain was bumpy and busy. I realized that Shirley Heights clearly was the place to be. After a short ride, we walked out on the mountaintop and gazed out over the harbor. Then it hit me: Jade. I remembered seeing this place in an image flash. She and I were facing each other, and as I looked beyond her, I could see two beautiful harbors. It was these harbors. This is where we will meet some day, I thought to myself. But in the flash she was older. Harry said she was 16 years old in the picture and that the picture was a year old. I also knew I would meet her at Reubens before I would see her here.

At that moment, Allen walked up and handed me a beer.

Antigua

"Michael, you look like you are very deep in thought."

"I'm just daydreaming."

"It's easy to do that up here. Have you ever seen anything so beautiful?"

"As a matter of fact, I have."

We stayed on Shirley Heights until darkness fell. The harbors lit up like a Christmas tree from the hundreds of anchor lights that glowed from the top of the mast heads. How lucky I felt to be standing there seeing such beauty and how sad I felt that the experience had to end. By 10:00 we motored back to the boat. By 10:30 we were all fast asleep.

In the Blink of an Eye

Chapter 36

Convergence of Events

Over the next 48 months, I had settled into a nice routine. Other than the trips to see Dr. Kim and hearing about the tumor, everything seemed to be going well. I kept myself busy writing my autobiography, working with Paul on the theater and every few months, traveling to Washington to spend time with Jodii at the temple. Allen and I had become closer than ever, spending time sailing on *Sea Pup*.

We made several other trips to the Caribbean, sailing in the Spanish Virgin Islands and Windward Islands. I was fit, sleeping well and seeing flashes that were simply a repeat of seeing Jade in South

In the Blink of an Eye

Africa and Shirley Heights. But like everything in life, the predictable is always somehow interrupted by the unpredictable. And in the back of my mind, I knew that some event was about to occur that would take me back to South Africa, where I would meet Jade at Reubens. That is when events started to converge.

The phone rang. "Hello."

"Hi, Michael."

"Hey Dad, what's up?"

"Great news."

"What? Tell me."

"I found a boat and I think I'm going to purchase it."

"What did you find?"

"It's a Beneteau 393."

"How old is she?"

"She's about 5 years old."

"Terrific. Where is she?"

"In one of your favorite places."

"The Caribbean?"

"Yes, but it's better than that."

"Antigua?"

"Exactly. Are you up for sailing her home with me and Mickey?"

"When?"

"Sixty to ninety days."

"Count me in."

Convergence of Events

That was event Number One.

A few days later, I got another call. This time it was from John Mac. The phone rang.

"Hello."

"Hi Michael, John here."

"John, how's it going?"

"Great. Did you get the distribution check?"

"Oh yeah, just like the last 60. How's Sinthis and the kids?"

"Everyone is well. Michael, we have a few issues at the marina."

"What's the problem?"

"We need to make some repairs to the sea wall and need an environmental permit. The regulators require that the owner be present at the permit hearing."

"When is the hearing?"

"It's in 10 days."

"Is there any other issue hanging out there?"

"Just one other."

"What's that?"

"Jade."

"Repeat that?"

"Jade, the girl you told me about. She applied for a job for a delivery crew."

"John, don't let her get away. I'll be on a plane to Cape Town in 48 hours."

"Okay. Have a safe trip."

In the Blink of an Eye

"Thanks and I'll keep you posted."

Thirty-six hours later I was boarding a plane at JFK Airport in New York, heading for Cape Town.

That was event Number Two.

For 14 hours I sat in my seat trying to stay focused on events that I believed would be unfolding. I was also trying to reconcile the cost of my first-class seat, which tipped the scale at just over $5,000. At the last moment, I decided not to book my return flight to Virginia but instead to Antigua. It looked like our departure from Antigua on Allen's new boat would occur within 30 days of my arrival in Cape Town. Between business in South Africa and relaxation in Antigua, I could easily consume a month. Of the 14 hours of air time, two hours were consumed by a "B" rated movie, eight were dedicated to updating my journal and autobiography, and the remaining four hours involved eating, drinking and thinking. The single issue spinning in my mind was on what day, and at what hour, would I meet Jade. I hoped that some sign would appear that would guide me to the specific moment when another piece of my future would be realized.

Our initial approach into Cape Town was consumed by confusion. First, the low altitude weather was ugly, with 30-knot winds and driving rain.

Convergence of Events

The flight attendant had dropped a tray of glasses that she had collected during our descent and there were two babies that started to scream from the apparent pain they were feeling in their ears from the change in cabin pressure. Then the lights in the first-class cabin started to flicker as if there was a short-circuit in the wiring.

Then it happened. I got blasted by five image flashes. Two of the flashes were of me talking to Jade. These flashes were from two vantage points. In the third flash, I could see my eyes. They were blue and brown. In the fourth flash, I could see a television set. There were two teams playing rugby. I could see the words Cape Town and Johannesburg. And in the last one, I could see an image of myself standing at Shirley Heights looking dazed and confused. I closed my eyes. I didn't want to see anymore.

The landing was thunderous as the plane slammed onto the runway. Several overhead storage compartments opened and a few small items fell out. Customs and immigration ended up being a very lengthy process. I felt over-interrogated and wondered why there were so many questions asked of me. When I arrived at the hotel, I found it empty and there was a strange feeling of stagnation. I walked to the gift shop, purchased a newspaper and reviewed the sports section. According to the paper, there was no rugby match between

In the Blink of an Eye

Cape Town and Johannesburg. Then I walked to the business center, logged onto the Internet and found the Web site for the Cape Town rugby team. There it was, Cape Town versus Johannesburg. The match was scheduled to occur five days from now.

The young girl at the registration desk stared at me as I approached the counter.

"Good afternoon."

"Hello, I have a reservation. The last name is Kenney."

"Let me check. Mr. Kenney, we have you in a junior suite, floor 12, room 10."

"Happy birthday," I said under my breath.

"I love your eyes, Mr. Kenney. Are they real or are you wearing contact lenses?"

"No, they're all mine."

"I had a dog that had eyes like you."

"I've heard others say that."

"I hope you enjoy your stay."

"Thanks, I'm sure I will."

After I unpacked, I called John. Connie answered the phone.

"Mac Delivery Service."

"Hi, Connie. Is John there?"

"Oh hello, Michael. How was your trip?"

"Okay; rough landing."

"Yeah, the weather here has been dreadful the last week. Let me get John."

John picked up the phone. "Michael, glad you

got in safe and sound. Are you coming over to the office?"

"No, I'm going to rest for awhile but I would like to get together tomorrow morning."

"Sure, boss."

"I want to see the repair work that needs to be done and I want to hear all the details about your inquiry from Jade."

"She seems like a nice kid. She's a bit green, however. I spoke with her yesterday. She is coming back for another interview in few days. I want her to meet the other crew members."

"Excellent."

"Did you know that she's a chef?"

"No, her father never said much about her. Very interesting. Anyway, I'll be over tomorrow at 9 a.m."

"Okay Michael, see you then."

A half-hour later the phone rang, waking me up from a light sleep.

"Hello, Michael. I didn't want to wake you but I just got a call from Jade. She is coming over here for an interview on Saturday at 10 a.m. I thought you would like to know."

"Interesting. That's the same day the rugby match is being played between Cape Town and Johannesburg."

"Okay, so what is the significance of that?"

"No significance. Thanks for letting me know.

In the Blink of an Eye

I'll see you tomorrow."

    "Great. See you then."

    Within minutes, I was in a deep sleep.

Chapter 37

Let the World Turn

The next day, I walked over to Mac Delivery Service with four things in mind. First was to get a better understanding of the needed repairs, and permitting process. Second was to prepare for the hearing. Third was to drop off bonus checks for John and his staff. And last was to determine whether I would listen in on the interview with Jade.

John and I toured the marina. A few sections of the sea wall needed replacing and some of the pier needed re-planking. John estimated that the repair would cost about $20,000. That was a small amount, considering that I had already recouped more than twice my original investment. There also was enough money in the bank account to pay for the repairs. So there was no problem there. Then John took me through the permitting process. As it turned out, my role in the hearing was minimal. I was there to testify that a completion bond would be secured and that a proper engineering firm would be hired to design the sea wall repair. All of this could've been done by letter, phone call or agent. However, I needed to be there anyway to fulfill my encounter with Jade.

John and I discussed the idea of me listening in on the interview.

"Michael, did you have a vision about being at the interview?"

"No."

"Then why do you want to be there?"

"I don't know. I think if I limit my discussion with her to our meeting at Reubens, that I will not get enough insight into why I am meeting her in the first place."

"Maybe there is not an important reason for the encounter."

"I also wondered about that, but Jodii told me that in his meditation, he envisioned something more than our two encounters."

"Two encounters?"

"Yes. I will see her again in Antigua."

"Are you sure?"

"Very sure."

Let the World Turn

"So what else did Monk Jodii say about the future?"

"He told me that I shouldn't take any more money from Mac Delivery Service. He told me that I had taken enough and that I had been repaid and that the profits should be shared with you."

"He didn't really say that, did he?"

"No, but that's what I'm going to do, right after the repairs are paid for. Use the money to put the twins through college."

"For real?"

"Yes, and give Connie a raise."

"Michael, you are a godsend."

"Give the kids a good education. It will be money well spent. So, back to Jade. What do you think I should do?"

"Let the world turn and don't mess with the Bujew."

"Are you saying I should stay away?"

"Yes, that's the advice of your employee."

"I'll take it under advisement."

On Friday morning we attended the permit hearing. Bill Fish, our contracted marine engineer, made a short presentation. John and I answered a few questions that were asked by the authorities. I paid the permitting fee, and returned to the hotel. On the way, I stopped by the bookstore and purchased two sailing magazines. I knew I would need them for Saturday night. Then I called John to let him know that I would be listening in on the interview.

I was startled by the sound of someone impatiently pounding on my hotel room door. I looked through the security peephole. There was a man standing at the door wearing a blue blazer. I could see a badge that he wore over his handkerchief pocket. It read "security." Behind him was another face. It was John. I opened the door. John spoke first.

"Michael, are you okay?"

"I think so."

"I was worried when you didn't show up this morning and never answered my phone calls." I looked over at the phone. The message light was flashing.

"What time is it?" I asked.

"It's four in the afternoon."

As John walked in the room, I noticed a strange feeling in my feet. I looked down and saw that my shoes were on backward. That I fixed immediately.

"Michael, what's going on?"

"I don't know. The last thing I remember I was lying in bed reading a sailing magazine. The next thing I remember is hearing the banging on the door." John walked to the bathroom.

"Well it looks like you or someone else showered, based on the towels that are lying in the tub." Then he walked over to the desk and picked up one of the composition notebooks. "What's this?"

He handed me the notebook. There were six pages of nonsensical scribble. The handwriting looked like it was done by a first grader. I collapsed in the chair. "Gosh, I must've been in a temporary demented state."

"Well, you were smart enough to order room service, but not smart enough to eat anything." The stainless steel cover had not been taken off the scrambled eggs and bacon that rested on the plate.

"John, it's the damn brain tumor. This is the first time I have been out of touch like this. I must've been sitting in this room all day and in a total daze."

"How do you feel now?"

"Just a little freaked out."

"I'll hang out for a while until both of us are sure you are okay." Then John walked over to the television, picked up the remote and started to surf until he found what he was looking for.

"Michael, do you like rugby?"

"I'm not that familiar with it."

"Well, there is a big match today; Cape Town Stormers vs. Johannesburg Blue Bulls."

In the Blink of an Eye

Chapter 38

The Encounter

John stayed until 7 p.m. and then left for home. After his departure, I walked over to Reubens. At the maitre d' stand was a tall young man. We made eye contact. He looked at me strangely. I looked back at him, waiting for him to make some comment about my eyes.

"Good evening. Do you have a reservation?"

"No."

"Will it be just you or are you expecting someone to join you?"

"It's just me."

"Okay, I can seat you."

"I would like a seat that has a good view of the

In the Blink of an Eye

bar." He walked me to my table.

"I hope you enjoy the evening."

"I'm sure I will."

"If there's anything I can do for you while you're at Reubens, let me know. My name is Andrew Peyton."

"Nice name. I'm Michael Kenney."

"Nice to meet you, Mr. Kenney."

"Andrew, why are the restaurant and bar so empty?"

"We tend to trade more on the business crowd and convention business. This time of year is a little slower."

A few minutes later, a waiter came to the table.

"Good evening, Mr. Kenney."

"Good evening."

"Would you like your martini as usual?"

"How do you know I want a martini?"

"Good guess. And would you like it on the rocks, dry and dirty?"

"Yes, very good. How did you know that?"

"I served you a martini five years ago in the bar."

"But how did you remember me and my drink preference?"

"It's your eyes. You're one in a billion. Plus, no one ever forgets a customer who gives a 100 percent tip."

The Encounter

"How did you know my name?"

"Andrew Peyton told me."

"Nice touch."

"Thanks. So what brings you to Reubens?"

"I am meeting someone here later on."

"Will she be joining you for dinner?"

"How do you know it's a she?"

"Lucky guess."

"No, I am meeting her in the bar."

"Shall I let Andrew Peyton know to expect her?"

"No, I don't know her name."

"Okay, then. Let me get the martini for you."

"Thanks."

The martini was followed by another martini which was then followed by a Caesar salad, roasted duck and cheesecake. By the time dinner was over, it was 10 p.m.

"Mr. Kenney, are you sure your date is going to meet you?" the waiter asked as he cleared the table.

"Yes, she will be here and she is not my date."

"Very well, sir."

"I think I'll move to the bar."

"Okay, I'll prepare your bill."

"Add another martini to the tab and deliver it to the bar."

"Right away, Mr. Kenney."

The bar was empty. My only company was the

In the Blink of an Eye

bartender and my sailing magazine. The martini sat in front of me. I decided I wouldn't touch it until Jade walked through the door. At 10:45, I glanced over the top of the magazine and looked outside. There she was, walking toward the entrance to Reubens. "Okay, Jade, what's on your mind?" I said in a whisper. She took a seat about midpoint on the L-shaped bar. She stared straight ahead, not noticing me. The bartender walked past me and winked as he walked over to Jade. She didn't look that different from the picture her father had shown me five years earlier. I continued to read my magazine. Every 15 seconds or so, I looked up to see what she was doing. My eyes shifted to the bartender. He picked up the vodka, poured it into a tumbler filled with ice, sprinkled a pinch of dry vermouth into the glass, and finished it off with two olives and a moderate portion of olive juice. "That's an interesting coincidence," I thought. Then he delivered the drink to Jade. She picked it up, swirled it and took a sip. Then she slid off the bar stool and started to walk toward me. I looked down at the magazine and waited. Butterflies formed in my stomach and my heartbeat started to race. "Here we go," I said to myself.

"Excuse me. I noticed you are reading a sailing magazine. Are you a sailor?" I swiveled my chair around in her direction. We made eye contact. She looked at me and was immediately taken aback.

The Encounter

"Yes, I sail on the Chesapeake Bay."

"Where's that?" she asked.

"In the U.S., East Coast, near Washington, D.C." Then I extended my hand and said, "Michael Kenney."

"How do you do, Mr. Kenney."

"Call me Michael."

"Very well. Michael."

"And your name?"

"Jade."

"Jade, nice to meet you." She reminded me of the age Audrey was when we met back in college. "So Jade, thinking of buying a boat?"

"No sir, but I'm about to crew on a Bluewater 46."

"Nice boat." Then she went on to tell me the whole story surrounding her impending trip. I listened very attentively.

She ordered another drink and then she asked, "Well, do you have any advice for me, Michael?" I took out my billfold and withdrew a small packet.

"Jade, I want you to have this. It is filled with colored sand. This sand was given to me by Paul Curry, a dear friend of mine, back in the States. This sand comes from a Buddhist mandala, a sand painting.

It has spiritual significance. It speaks of life's impermanence. The Tibetan monks who created this mandala did so as part of a prayer ritual. The

In the Blink of an Eye

mandala is beautiful, and the effort that goes into its creation is immense. Shortly after the mandala is completed, it is destroyed. This is done to illustrate life's impermanence and to recognize that death is a part of life. They believe in reincarnation, as I do. You must carry it with you for the rest of your life. The sand will guide you.

"Jade, there are 13 things you must remember. I will assume that your Judeo-Christian upbringing gave you 10; the sand will guide you to two of them. I will give you one. The first 10 are the Ten Commandments. Modernize them as you wish. Numbers 11 and 12 come from the sand. You are in search of a new beginning. You are in search of inner peace. Inner peace can only come from the convergence of wisdom and compassion. When you don't know what to do, place the sand in your hand and remember: be wise, make your decisions carefully, use logic, not emotion. Be compassionate, think about others, make sure you understand how your decisions will affect others, look for the best in others and seek to understand before you seek to be understood.

"And number 13, I call the Platinum Rule. Do unto others as they would want done to themselves. Do not presuppose you know what is right for someone else. Godspeed, Jade."

She looked at her drink and noticed it was empty. She continued to stare for what felt like 30

The Encounter

seconds, and at that moment, I realized it was my cue to leave. I moved off the bar stool, took my drink and napkin and walked back into the restaurant, and out of her visual line of sight. I kept my eyes on her for a few seconds until she picked up her head and noticed I was gone. She had a look on her face that said, "Where did he go; did I just see a ghost?" She looked around the bar, then looked behind her and started to walk toward the restaurant's entrance. I slipped out the front door and walked quickly down the street and into the hotel. From the lobby I looked out at Reubens entrance. A few minutes later Jade walked out, got in her car and drove away.

In the Blink of an Eye

Chapter 39

Out of Africa

The next few days that followed were peaceful. I felt very satisfied with my encounter with Jade and was looking forward to finishing up my work at Mac Delivery Service, and then heading off to Antigua. On the last day of my visit I had dinner with John and Sinthis. Their home was not too far from Scarborough Beach. It was a joyful dinner until the end. Sinthis then looked at me.

"I guess this is the end, Michael, isn't it?"

"What do you mean?"

"Your work is done here. You found the next piece of your puzzle, your illness is progressing and you really don't have any reason to come back

In the Blink of an Eye

here." A tear rolled down her cheek.

I grabbed her hand. "I guess you're right." Now tears were rolling down my cheeks as well.

"Michael, it doesn't have to be this way."

"I'm afraid it does. I'm running out of time and I need to move on." Sinthis moved close to me and hugged me. I could feel her tears on my shoulder. I momentarily felt like Jost. I looked down at her to make sure she wasn't Sonnet.

"John, take good care of your family. I'll call you next week. Keep me abreast of the progress the crew is making. Make sure the guys take good care of Jade. If anything happens, I want to know. Just leave a message on my cell phone."

"I will. Michael, thanks for everything."

"No, thank you, John and remember, don't send me any more checks."

"Are you sure?"

"Totally sure." I turned and walked toward the door and made my way to the rental car.

John yelled out, "Michael, enjoy your sail with your dad." I didn't reply. I just raised my hand in the air and displayed a "thumbs up."

The next morning as I was boarding the plane to Antigua, Jade was boarding *Renovatio*, the boat she and the other crew members would be delivering to the British Virgin Islands. I wasn't sure what was going to happen while en route that would make them change their plans from the British Virgin Islands to Antigua, but I decided to leave that to a higher power to resolve.

The most direct flight from Cape Town to Antigua was through Paris on Air France, followed by a flight to Sint Maarten and then from Sint Maarten to Antigua. In order to avoid Sint Maarten, I had booked Cape Town to London, London to Bermuda, Bermuda to Puerto Rico, and Puerto Rico to Antigua. The flight, including layovers, would take 28 hours. The one positive was that I would have 28 hours to work on my autobiography, which was now up to date.

My seat in first class was spacious and the person next to me didn't speak English, so I knew I was in for a quiet flight. The first order of business was to document in detail every step I needed to take over the next few days just in case I had a memory lapse or a repeat of the events of the previous Saturday morning.

The 28-hour flight seemed to go by faster than I'd expected. I slept much more than I had thought I would and therefore, didn't get much done editing my autobiography. After I retrieved my bags and cleared customs, I took a cab to the hotel. I asked the registration clerk if Allen Stern had arrived yet, and he indicated that he had.

As it turned out, the boat Allen was purchasing required a fair amount of work before she would be ready for the 1,500-mile trip from Antigua to

In the Blink of an Eye

Virginia. Allen had allowed three weeks to get the boat prepared. The timeframe also coincided with the date that Mick Dermott would be arriving to join us. After unpacking, I called Allen's room but nobody answered, so I took a cab to the marina to check in on Allen's progress. When I arrived, Allen was in the midst of changing out most of the running rigging.

"Dad," I yelled out. Allen turned around.

"Michael, welcome to English Harbour. How was your trip?"

"It was long but I'm here."

"Anything new in Cape Town?"

"Nothing unexpected."

"Well, come aboard, let me show you around." I walked onto the boat.

"What's her name?"

"*Ra-el*."

"I wonder what that means?"

"It was the name of the person for whom the boat was named."

"Hey, I thought I was the family wiseguy. Are you thinking about changing the name?"

"I don't know. Do you have any suggestions?"

"How about *Breezehound*?"

"Why *Breezehound*?"

"I don't know. I thought it would go well with *Sea Pup*."

"Well, for now, I think I'll stick with *Ra-el*."

Out of Africa

"How is the to-do list going?"

"I have a couple more weeks of work and could really use your help."

"Well Dad, I'm looking forward to getting my hands dirty."

"Great."

Over the next week we worked on the engine, replaced some electronics and completed a general inspection of all of the plumbing and electrical systems. As I was changing the engine oil, my cell phone rang, indicating I had a message. I dialed voicemail and listened to the message.

"Hi Michael, I hope all is going well. I just got a call from the crew. They have arrived in Salvador, Brazil. There have been a few autopilot problems but other than that, things appear to be going well. Jade has been doing a good job on board but did get a small laceration on her chin during some bad weather. The guys said she's been a real trooper. They will be staying in Salvador for a few days before they head to the BVIs. I'll keep you posted."

Allen looked at me. "Long message, wasn't it?"

"Yeah, it was John from Cape Town. He was calling me about a boat delivery that I am particularly interested in."

"What's your interest?"

"There's a young girl on board who is the cook. I met her father briefly in Cape Town. I was inter-

In the Blink of an Eye

ested to see how she was doing. That's all."

Day after day we worked on the to-do list. The list was getting shorter and I was getting concerned that Allen would want to leave as soon as Mick Dermott arrived. I needed to figure out what stall tactics I would use to keep us in Antigua long enough for me to meet Jade on Shirley Heights.

As the next week came to a close, Mick Dermott arrived. Because of his schedule, we needed to be underway in a few days for the 10-day sail back to Virginia. That night, while at dinner with Allen and Mick Dermott, the cell phone rang again. This time I was able to answer it before it rolled to voicemail. It was John.

"Hello, John?" There was a slight delay.

"Michael, how are you?"

"All is well. What's new in Cape Town?"

"Everything is fine. I got a call from the crew. They're in Trinidad. The auto pilot has failed and they need to replace the system. That's the bad news. The good news is that they found a replacement auto pilot in Antigua. They're going to sail there, get the vessel fixed, and then another crew will deliver the boat to BVIs. So Michael, go meet Jade and complete the next piece of the puzzle."

"John, this is big news." And at that moment, I lost the cell phone connection.

Chapter 40

Shirley Heights

We were just two days from departure and I was becoming concerned that I might have to leave Antigua and would miss Jade. We were all busy provisioning *Ra-el*, and Allen had made arrangements with the customs officials for clearance out of Antigua within 48 hours. As I carried the last box of groceries to the boat, my cell phone rang indicating that there was another voicemail.

"Michael, John here. I just wanted you to know that I got a call from the crew. They are docked at Bluewater's pier in Falmouth Harbour. Good luck." I made a short walk from our slip to Bluewater's dock. I started walking down the vari-

In the Blink of an Eye

ous piers until I came upon a catamaran that fit the description of the boat Jade was sailing. I looked across from one pier to another and saw the name *Renovatio* on the stern of the white catamaran. I returned to *Ra-el* to find Allen and Mick Dermott sitting in the cockpit.

"So Michael, we should be ready to leave in the morning."

"Is there any chance we could consider a one-day delay?"

"Why?"

"I have some business I need to take care of with the delivery crew that just delivered one of John's boats to Antigua."

"I think Mick and I would prefer to leave to-morrow but if we have to delay one day, I guess we can do that."

"I would really appreciate it and it would help me out a lot."

"Mick, is that okay with you?" Allen asked.

"I think I can take another day in paradise."

When Sunday arrived, I was especially anxious because I knew I had one chance to complete the next piece of the puzzle. At 5 p.m. I walked up the long road to Shirley Heights. The heat had been especially intense the last few days and my face had gotten quite sunburned. By the time I had gotten to Shirley Heights I was hot, sweaty and tired. I paid my entrance fee, passed through the bar, picked up

Shirley Heights

a beer and walked out on Shirley Heights. The sun was hanging low in the sky, so I lowered my hat to shade my eyes and put on my sunglasses.

As I consumed the beer, I became quite confused. I started asking myself why I was on Shirley Heights and why I was not back on the boat with Allen and Mick Dermott. I reached into my pocket to pull out the piece of paper that detailed the events of the day, but the paper was not there. I continued to search for the reason why I was alone on Shirley Heights without Allen and Mick Dermott. There must've been a reason but at that moment, I could not seem to put my finger on it. I grew frustrated and agitated and was starting to consider leaving Shirley Heights when a young girl turned to me.

"Excuse me. Would you mind snapping a quick picture of me and my friends?"

"Be glad to. Big smiles." The picture was taken. "Stay there, let me take another. Got it."

"Thanks."

I handed her the camera and walked toward the exit. Once there, I grabbed a cab and returned to English Harbour. When I arrived, I walked back to the boat. Allen and Mick Dermott were nowhere to be found. I searched through my cabin and found the piece of paper that should have been in my pocket. There was a note on it that said "go to Shirley Heights to meet Jade." I collapsed on

In the Blink of an Eye

my bunk and started to mumble to myself. "Was that Jade whose picture I took? That girl didn't look like her, but it must have been. How could I have missed such an important opportunity or was it meant to happen this way?" The next thing I knew, I woke up, looked at my watch and realized it was 11 p.m. I left the boat and walked toward Falmouth Harbour.

The streets leading to Falmouth Harbour were lined with restaurants and cafés that catered to the cruising crowd. I decided to stop in one of the bars for a drink. I ordered a beer and sat at the bar looking out at the crowd. The bar was full of young people, some of which were engaged in karaoke while others played pool. I reached into my pocket and pulled out a packet of sand. I stared at the sand and thought to myself, why am I here? There must be a reason.

At that moment, I looked up and saw the girl from Shirley Heights. She had just laid the microphone down and was walking over to the pool table. I realized at that moment that it was Jade. I stared up toward the ceiling and noticed the paddles of the ceiling fan turning slowly. I blinked and caught an image of myself walking out of the café and while doing so, pulling out a packet of sand and slipping it into Jade's pocket. I thought about whether I should comply with my vision and decided to fulfill what I had seen. The execution

Shirley Heights

was perfect. I passed by the crowded pool table and slipped a packet of sand into her pocket. She never felt the thing.

When I returned to the boat, Allen and Mick Dermott were in their bunks fast asleep. I took out a piece of paper and composed the following letter.

Dear Jade,

Once again, we meet for only a brief moment, before some event calls us to different directions. We obviously didn't recognize each other when I took your picture the other day. You look quite different. Very fit, I might add.

Things have become very complicated for me. I would have liked to stay in Antigua but my boat was leaving early in the morning and I needed to start my journey back home. You see, life comes at you quickly. Sometimes you can dodge a bullet and sometimes you can't. All I can tell you is that I believe we will meet again. Where and when, I don't know, but time is of the essence. While my future is clear, yours is not. There are many things I wish to share with you but that will have to wait until our next meeting.

By the way, I slipped the sand into your pocket at Nick's last night, when you were shooting pool. I didn't want to break your concentration. And by the way, karaoke is not your thing.

In the Blink of an Eye

I trust that the 13 principles have treated you well. How is the Bujew? If you ever get to Hampton Roads, Virginia, look me up, and if not, have a wonderful life.

Michael Kenney

After the letter was complete, I folded it in thirds, sealed with a single staple and walked back to the marina where *Renovatio* was docked. Once there, I slid the letter into the mail slot at the Bluewater marina office. I walked back to the boat, climbed into my bunk and fell asleep. By 6 a.m. the next day, we were motoring out of English Harbour on our way home.

Chapter 41

Homeward Bound

The next 10 days of my life were spent at sea. Those days represented the very best of life and the very worst of life. The very best was the sailing. For most of the trip we had winds out of the east blowing at 15 to 20 knots. The ocean was kind to us with 4- to 6-foot rolling seas. It was easy sailing most of the time. On occasion we ran through a moderate squall that only lasted 10 minutes or so. We had time to read and relax and in my case, write. It was only on rare occasions that we ran the engine and that was strictly for the purpose of topping off the batteries.

As to the very worst of life, it was only me who

In the Blink of an Eye

had to experience this. Shortly after we left English Harbour, I began to have a series of severe headaches. This followed with seasickness that should not have really occurred, given our constant pleasant conditions. I felt better at night than I did during the day, so we decided to adjust the watch schedule, giving me the opportunity to sleep most of the day and to take watch most of the night.

Sitting alone in the cockpit doing nothing but watching the darkness could easily drive a man crazy. But for me, it was a retreat and a place to get away from my illness. I spent a lot of time thinking about Jade and how she might impact the remainder of my life. I had a sense that the tumor was growing more rapidly and that my days on earth were dwindling.

Somewhere in the middle of the Atlantic Ocean during one of my night watches, I wandered back to a dangerous place. I started to feel self-pity and anger. I asked myself the same question over and over again; why me, why Jost? Then I started second-guessing all the important decisions I had made in my life. I found myself dwelling on the events in Sint Maarten with Audrey and wondered if I had made a significant mistake. On another night, I sat in the darkness for hours, never checking the instruments or the charts. And on another night, I thought about slipping over the side and putting an end to my meaningless life.

Homeward Bound

Several days later we pulled into Hampton. Su was there to greet us. She seemed very relieved to know that her family was back on dry land. It took the next few days to unpack *Ra-el* and to clean her up. After the chores were complete, I spent the next few days catching up on all the mail and paying all the bills that piled up during the six weeks I was gone. I also had to go see the doctor for another assessment of my disease. Once again, I climbed into the tube of the MRI and then listened to Dr. Kim comment on the growth of the tumor. Only this time, Dr. Kim was more definitive than in the past. This time my life expectancy was expressed not in years, but rather in months.

I determined that the most important thing for me to accomplish was to try and figure out the remaining pieces of the puzzle. I knew from my earlier flashes that Jade would visit me one more time, but when she did, it would be after my death. I knew that the answers to the rest of the puzzle lay in the flashes.

For the next two days, I stayed in my room, focused on the blades of the fan. Piece by piece I saw my future emerge. I was both stunned by what I saw but also pleased with the conclusion of my life. There was some reason and some logic behind my illness, and knowing this made me less concerned with death. I felt nearly complete now that the riddle had been solved. But my completeness was

In the Blink of an Eye

tainted by the one remaining and lingering regret.

In the weeks that followed, I managed to finish the manuscript of my autobiography. I printed one copy and placed it in a manila envelope. On the envelope I wrote the name of the autobiography. The envelope would be given to Paul at the right moment. Then I sat down at the kitchen table and wrote to Jade.

I took the letter, folded it in thirds and sealed it with a single staple. Then I laid it beside the manuscript and called Paul Curry.

Part Three
According to Paul

In the Blink of an Eye

Chapter 42

The Great Deception

No one could have asked for a better friendship than I had with Michael Kenney. And yet I had willingly chosen to deceive him. There were so many times he would ask me if things were okay, as he could sense uneasiness in our relationship.

It started seven years ago upon his return from his initial trip to Sint Maarten. There were so many times I wanted to tell him about the deception but somehow, I was unable to do so. On so many occasions, I attempted to stop the deception but each time decided to keep the secret from him. And now I was about to do it again.

Like the first Sunday of every month, I picked

In the Blink of an Eye

up the phone and made the phone call. And like the first Sunday of every month, the person on the other end waited to receive my phone call. The phone rang three times before it was answered.

"Hello?"

"Hi, how are you doing?"

"Never mind me, how is he doing?"

"He went to see the doctor last week and the news is not good." There was a long pause.

"What does 'not good' mean?"

"From what Michael said, the doctor gave him about six months." There was another long pause. Then I could hear crying.

"That's it; I'm coming home."

"Are you sure you want to do this?"

"I've never been so sure of anything in my life."

"Let me forewarn you that he's not the same man you remember. The disease has been tough on him."

"Frankly, I don't care; I'm tired of being half a person."

"When should I expect you?"

"I'll be there within a week."

"Be careful and have a safe trip."

"I will. Paul, thanks for everything."

"No problem."

Five minutes later the phone rang.

The Great Deception

"East Mellen Street Theater."

"Paul, it's Michael."

"How are you doing, old friend?"

"Not bad for a dead man walking. Is there a chance you could come by the apartment this afternoon?"

"Yes, I should be able to stop by around four o'clock. Is anything wrong?"

"No. I've just started to get my things in order and I have something I want to give you for safekeeping."

"Well, tell me what it is?"

"You'll find out when you get here."

"OK. I'll see you at four."

The drive over to Queen Street took longer than normal. I parked the car near Michael's yellow sports car and walked up the stairs to his apartment. When I got there, the door was opened, so I walked in. Michael was standing in the living room. His back was facing me. He was staring out the window as if in a trance. I walked over to him and put my hand on his shoulder. He didn't move. "Thanks for coming over, Paul. I really appreciate it."

"Anytime." He grabbed his cane which was leaning on the window sill and slowly walked toward the kitchen.

"Michael, are you in any pain?"

"No, not really. I just have been having a few

In the Blink of an Eye

issues with my balance. Paul, do you know how long I've lived in this apartment?"

"Has it been 20 years or so?"

"Not that long, but it's been probably 15 years."

"That's a long time to be renting."

"I know. Do you know how many sails have been made in this building over the last 15 years?"

"No, Michael, I don't."

"More than enough for me to have sailed from Hampton to Sint Maarten a hundred times. I really love living here, so close to the sail loft. It's one of the things I will really miss." I said nothing. Then he walked to the table and picked up the envelope. On top of the envelope was a folded piece of paper. Michael picked it up and handed it to me.

"Paul, there is a letter here for a girl named Jade. Sometime after my death, she will come looking for me at the theater. I want you to give her the letter. In the envelope is the manuscript of my autobiography. I want you to see that it gets published. Make sure copies get distributed to my family and friends. I picked up the envelope and looked at the writing on the cover. Then I opened the envelope and removed the manuscript. It was titled "In the Blink of an Eye."

Chapter 43

The Arrival

She stood in the lobby of the theater waiting for me to come down from the second-floor office. She was taller than I thought she would be and clearly more beautiful. She wore a light blue cotton sleeveless blouse and a white linen skirt. Her blonde hair was pulled back into a ponytail. I walked toward her and extended my hand.

"Paul, it's so nice to meet you after all these years." We hugged briefly.

"How was your flight?"

"It was fine, but I have to tell you, I've never been so nervous in my life. How is he doing?"

"When I saw him a few days ago, I noticed he

was walking with a cane."

"Is that new?"

"Yes, he said he'd been having some issues with his balance."

"Have you told him anything about me coming here?"

"No, I haven't said a word."

"Can you drive me over there?"

"No problem. Let me run up to the office and get my keys." I returned to the lobby, grabbed her bag and walked to my car.

"How long is the drive over to Michael's?"

"Ten minutes or so."

We made the short drive over to Queen Street. I noticed her foot tapping on the floor mats.

"Are you okay?"

"Yes, but I'm a nervous wreck."

We parked the car on the street and walked up the stairs to Michael's apartment. I knocked on the door. I could hear his footsteps as he approached the door. I moved to the side, putting Audrey in front of me. I could hear the lock tumblers move. Then the door opened slowly. Michael stood there. He was motionless and speechless.

"Michael, it's me." Then he dropped his cane and walked toward her. At that moment I turned around and walked down the stairs. As I left the building, I could hear him say, "Audrey, I love you."

The Arrival

For the next few weeks, I didn't hear anything from either Michael or Audrey. I had thought about calling him but instead decided to call Su. Our phone call was brief. She told me that she had spoken to Michael and that it seemed as if new life had been breathed into him. She also said that he had been to see Mickey Dermott but that Mickey would not disclose to her the nature of his visit.

A few days later, I got a call from Jodii. He was inquiring about Michael's health and was concerned that he had not heard from him in several weeks. I gave Jodii an update on all the events that occurred and told him that if I spoke to Michael, I would have him call.

Finally, I got up the nerve to call him. The phone rang several times until it rolled to voice-mail. "You've reached the Kenney residence. Sorry we are not home right now but if you leave a message, we will call you back as soon as we can." I left a brief message and hung up the phone. Then I smiled, having realized that the recording on his answering machine referred to "we" instead of "I."

Several days later I got a return call from Michael.

"East Mellen Street Theater."

"Hi Paul, it's Michael."

"Michael, how are you and how's Audrey?"

"Things have been perfect. I found a whole

In the Blink of an Eye

new level of happiness."

"I'm really happy for you, my old friend."

"I wanted to let you know that I got a call from Jodii and he's coming down this weekend. Would you be available to join us for a sail on Allen's boat?"

"Absolutely! I wouldn't miss it for the world."

"Great. Meet at the marina at 10 in the morning on Saturday."

"I'll be there."

On Saturday morning, I drove down to the marina. Everyone was on board when I arrived. I climbed on deck and we were soon underway. The wind on the bay was perfect. The sky was clear and the warm sun shined on us. Michael took the helm. Audrey sat beside him. I could feel the energy of two people so deeply in love and wondered why it took them nearly 20 years to come together.

The sailing continued for several hours and during that time, there were few words spoken. I think all of us would have preferred to have been somewhere else so that Michael and Audrey could be alone. But in a strange way, I think Michael wanted us to see him and remember him in the happiest moments of his life. He was now complete and a full person, having not only resolved his past and his future, but also his present.

Chapter 44

Remembrance

It was a bright sunny day as we filed into the small church just off East Mellen Street. I thought it was strange that Michael had selected this church for his memorial service. But why not? After all, this was where he was to be buried. The church was packed with people from the community. I had not realized how many people Michael Kenney had touched in his short life.

Jodii stood at the altar of the church beside Father Delao. Jodii spoke:

"Death is inevitable. There are two ways of dealing with death. First is simply to try to avoid the problem, to put it out of your mind, even

In the Blink of an Eye

though the reality of the problem is still there. The other way of dealing with death is to look at it directly, analyze it, make it familiar and to make it a part of your life. Whether we like it or not, death is bound to occur. Don't avoid thinking about it, but rather choose to understand it. Michael was my brother. In life there are a few people who deserve that distinction. He was a man who cared deeply about the welfare of others. He was a generous person whose love had no boundaries. The goodness he created in the world can be seen through the ways he extended both his hand and his heart to others. The world would have been a better place if he stayed with us longer but that was simply not to be. ..."

Jodii's eulogy continued for a few more minutes. Then Audrey walked up to the altar.

"Good morning. My name is Audrey Kenney. I consider myself one of the luckiest women on earth. For most of my life, I lived with regrets. I've known for more than 20 years that I loved Michael more than I ever loved anyone else. But for reasons that are no longer relevant, it took 20 years for Michael and me to realize how much we loved each other.

"In the years that we were apart, there was not one day that I did not tell myself that I loved him. And as he told me, there was not one day in his life that he did not say to himself that he loved me.

Remembrance

Somewhere in all this is a lesson about love and the need for people to express to each other their true feelings."

"These last five months that Michael and I were together were the most wonderful five months of our lives. And as we say goodbye to Michael, my husband, and our child's father, I only wish that our child grows up to be the same thoughtful, giving and loving person that Michael was.

"There are two people here, and you know who you are, who should be honored for the job they did raising their adopted son, Michael. Michael requested that if our child is a boy, that he be named Allen Stern Kenney. And if our child is a girl, that she be named Su Stern Kenney. This is a wish of Michael's I will carry out. Michael, I know you can hear me, and you know each day I will tell you what I have said to you every day of my adult life, and that is simply that I love you."

After Audrey spoke, there was very little that could be said that would have changed the mood of everyone in the church. Then Father Delao spoke briefly about Michael's generosity toward the church. As he finished his comments, I noticed a strange curiosity on the faces of Su and Allen. Michael obviously had not told them about the gift he had made.

After the memorial service was over, we went to

In the Blink of an Eye

the cemetery. I escorted Audrey to the cemetery as we walked through the narrow spaces between the old tombstones. As we approached the two graves-ites next to Michael, Audrey stopped, bowed her head and prayed over the stones of Angel Lehcar and Jost Alexson. Then Michael's body was carried to the gravesite and lowered into the ground. Jodii said a few more words about death being a part of life and then Allen shoveled three scoops of earth onto the coffin in the Hebrew tradition.

And so ended the life of Michael Kenney, a person who will always be my friend.

Chapter 45

The Third Meeting

The monks were in residency at the East Mellen Street Theater. It was the third day of their visit and the wisdom mandala was near completion. Jodii and I were standing in the lobby talking with the various visitors who came to see the beautiful sand paintings. As I looked across the lobby, I made eye contact with the young woman. She looked to be about 25 years old. She had long brown hair and she walked with a purposeful stride. She walked over to me.

"Excuse me. I'm looking for Michael Kenney or a person named Curry. Do you know either of them?"

In the Blink of an Eye

"I'm Paul Curry. You must be Jade. I suppose you are here to see Michael."

"Yes, do you know where he is?"

"Yes, I see him every day. I will take you to him, but first I must get something from my office.

Stay right here." I walked up to my office and retrieved the letter. Then I walked down and signaled her to follow me. We walked out a side door, down an alley and onto the street.

"He is just around the corner. So, how has the-sand treated you, Jade of South Africa?" She said nothing. "Here we are."

"Where? He lives in a church?"

"No, he lives over there." I extended my arm and pointed to the church's cemetery. "This is Michael Kenney's new home. He died two weeks ago." She started to collapse. I grabbed her under her arm to steady her. Tears poured down her face. She looked empty and lifeless as if a part of her was dying.

"Jade." My voice startled her. "Walk with me."

We walked; her knees were shaking. We stopped in front of the stone.

"Curry, this stone looks to be hundreds of years old. Have others been buried here?" She tried to make out the other names but the engravings had been filled in with mortar.

Then I helped her down to her knees and handed her the letter.

The Third Meeting

"Michael knew you'd be coming someday. He told me he didn't know when but he was sure that you would be coming." I walked away. She sat there crying as if she had just lost a very close friend.

She opened the letter and read it aloud.

Dear Jade,

So we missed each other this time. My loss. The sand you have carried is a reminder of life's impermanence. The monks create a mandala in honor of life and prayer and shortly thereafter destroy it, to demonstrate life's fragility.

We Buddhists do not fear death. Death is a part of life. We are all reincarnated over and over again. It's a circle, not too different from the circle you and I have created. I found you in Cape Town and now you have found me. Continue your dreams, and your adventure. Someday you will fall in love. You will have children and you will return to Cape Town.

Everything that has occurred in this life has been for the sole purpose of our final meeting. The day I met your father many years ago, and our two meetings, are all part of a much larger plan. While all of this may be very confusing to you, someday it will make perfect sense as we will learn to love each other in ways you cannot imagine. This is our destiny.

Have a wonderful life, Jade, of South Africa.

In the Blink of an Eye

Sincerely,
Michael Kenney.

She continued to kneel by the grave for several minutes until she looked up at me and asked me if I knew what the letter meant.

"Jade, somehow you and Michael are connected in a special way and someday you will understand the significance of this letter. My advice to you is to get on with your life, follow your dreams, and someday all that has happened to you today will make perfect sense." She stood up and wiped the tears from her eyes. We walked back to the theater and then I walked Jade to her car.

"Jade, I want you to do me a favor."

"Sure, what is it?"

"Here's my card; keep in touch with me. I think that's what Michael would have wanted."

Two months later Michael's will was settled. Most of the money was left in trust for the baby. Mac Delivery Service was held by a separate trust for five years, at which time it was to be transferred to Michael's other heir. Over the next five years, I received letters and postcards from Jade. She had found a man named James and had fallen in love. After five years of traveling they settled in South Africa, at which time the trust transferred the ownership of Mac Delivery Service to her and her hus-

The Third Meeting

band. The last communication I received from Jade was about the birth of her child. Jade and James had a baby girl named Ruby M. Morison. Jade told me that the M. was in honor of Michael. Enclosed in the letter was a photograph of Jade's baby. I stared at the photograph and felt a sense of closure. The baby had one blue eye and one brown eye.